S0-DUS-010

"I would just like to say one thing about this book."
LISA BOBOCHEK,
Australian Sheepshearers' Association Ladies' Auxiliary

"A heartwarming tale about a boy and his mom."
FELICIA SHADROE,
Aspen *Crier*

"If this is the key to the information superhighway, then we're in for a rough ride."
SENATOR LANCE BOYLE,
Chairman, Senate Paving Committee, U.S. Senate

"A cool read."
W. 'SHARK' WINFIELD

"Unutterable trash."
K. SALAMON

"The author has a unique talent for rendering comprehensible the maunderings of the savants and other denizens of the high-technology world."
NOAH WEBSTER

"Buy this book, if you know what's good for you."
NICK FALOTTI

a satirical romance

# DOWN IN THE VALLEY

## Bill Schaffer

TEMBLOR PRESS

The author wishes to acknowledge the invaluable assistance of the following people: Susan Patricelli and Linda Brown for reviewing the manuscript, and Klaus Hofmann, John Pescatore, Sarah Smith and Gesine Schaffer for their many helpful comments.

This is a work of fiction. The companies, characters, and situations are the product of the author's fevered imagination.

Text and cover designed and produced by David Bullen
Cover art by Leslie Silva

FIRST EDITION

ISBN 0-9641498-6-9
LIBRARY OF CONGRESS CATALOG CARD NUMBER: 94-090226

10  9  8  7  6  5  4  3  2  1


Temblor Press
26030A Highland Way
Los Gatos, CA  95030

To A.R.S.

*pro fidem tuam*

Persons attempting to find a
motive in this narrative will be
prosecuted.     *Mark Twain*

# DOWN
## IN THE
# VALLEY

# prologue

I STOOD IN THE corridor of Building Nine of Data-Drive, Inc., clutching my sheaf of overheads, and trying to keep my knees from knocking. The Executive Committee was meeting on the other side of the wall. These were the guys—they were all men, as was usual in the Valley—who ran the whole show. From the sounds that penetrated the large glass window, shielded by drawn blinds, ExCom was in an angry, even hungry, mood. I knew from whispered reports that these meetings could be as terrible for the low-level employee unfortunate enough to be a part of the agenda as were the conclaves in the Roman coliseum, where innocent slaves and Christians were served up as the menu of the day to ferocious beasts. The kindest description I had heard of the ExCom meetings was "dysfunctional." And shortly I was to appear as the star witness, representing the fate of six hundred men and women, footsoldiers of the company, who had dedicated the last ten months of their lives to Project Nemo.

Between waves of fear, I was in a reflective state. How had it happened that I, whose only exposure to the world of high technology had been the purchase of an elaborate Japanese toaster a couple of years ago, was about to address some of the smartest people in the industry? It was like the nightmare actors have when they find themselves on a stage, with about four thousand people in the hushed audience, and have never once read the script. Only I wasn't in a nightmare. Or at least, not the kind where you scream once or twice and then wake up.

None of this would have happened if I hadn't had to pee in such a bad way about three months back. And I couldn't help thinking that that fateful urging of the bladder—well, to be honest, it was more of a clarion call—wouldn't have occurred if I hadn't been so obsessed with a spate of articles about enlarged prostates that seemed to have afflicted the local press around two years ago, back in Terre Haute, where I used to hail from. It seems that one of the symptoms of enlarged prostates is an intense need to pee. I mean pee right then and there, as it were....

## one

CARMELITA, THE RECEPTIONIST at Building Fifteen, sat at her workstation clicking her fingernails on the keyboard, but not typing anything. She was worried because she hadn't heard from her boyfriend in over a week. She felt that somehow she had lost control over Kurt, and she didn't like losing control at all. As she had just said to Trudi, the floater, who was sitting behind her unraveling some knitting and waiting for Carmelita to go off to lunch, "It isn't that he's the greatest guy in the world, because he's not. But God, I mean I practically left home for his sake. My Dad finds out I'm dating a non-Hispanic, I mean if he *was* someone, OK, but Kurt? I mean, 'who is he?' says my father."

Trudi knew what she meant. Her own father was difficult, though of course Trudi had never had a problem with a cross-cultural relationship. Trudi hadn't had any relationships at all, not even a problematic one, and here she was, twenty-two years old, no guy, and still inching her way through college two courses at a clip. With the need to earn tuition it was all she could do to keep up with the two. Things were not better on the job front, either. She wasn't even a full-time contract employee, but just a temp, and a floater at that. She didn't have a lot of friends because she had gone to high school in Modesto until her parents had finally split and she had come to the Bay area to stay with her father. She could make that decision because her mother hadn't particularly cared where Trudi ended up. Her brother elected to stay in Modesto, first because he had just started high school and didn't want to leave his friends, and second because he hated his father for some reason Trudi didn't know, nor was she terribly interested. Her father basically left her to her own devices, except that he would only allow her to stay for free in the house in Sunnyvale if she kept on being a student in good standing at college and stayed employed.

Her father had a girlfriend, of course. "Which is really grotesque!" Trudi had said to Carmelita one day. "Because my Dad is fifty-six, and then he brings this girl, this bimbette, to the house one night and she gives me a look like she was wondering what I was doing there! My Dad goes, 'This is my daughter Trudi.' And she goes, 'Well, hi there!' and she just smiles at me, and I see she's like my own age, for God's sake! Or younger! I mean, what is a kid like that doing with a fifty-six-year-old insurance agent?"

"You know what she's doing," Carmelita had said. "Help me with these FedEx packages. The guy's due here any minute for the pickup."

Trudi might have been only a floater, but she was a good kid and not afraid to help out, even when break time was over and the regular girl or guy was back on station. Technically she should now be having her break, but she liked Carmelita, who was a listener, if not always sympathetic the way Trudi would have liked. She grabbed a stack of FedEx forms. "I still don't get it," she said after a while. "This girl is living with my Dad! And I'm tiptoeing around the house when I get back after school because even though it's only a little after nine, the two of them are there in the bedroom and I feel so funny, I don't want her to know I'm in the house. It's real weird. I mean it's beyond far out."

"What's her name?" asked Carmelita.

"Who knows?" Trudi said sulkily.

"You don't know her name?" Carmelita said, incredulous.

"Yeah, I do. It's Terry. Short for Teresa."

"Oh," said Carmelita. She found this interesting. "Is she Hispanic?"

"Her last name is Yamaguchi," said Trudi. "So I doubt it."

At this point the phone gurgled at Carmelita. All the phones at DataDrive were state of the art, of course, and so the phones couldn't just ring or buzz. They had to make a sound like Carmelita's five-year-old brother made when he burbled into his glass of Coke at dinner to get his mother mad. And these phones showed who was calling; there was a little screen on which the name of the caller popped up, so the person called could decide whether or not to pick it up. Carmelita knew about the little power games that could be played by anyone with these phones. At DataDrive, as elsewhere in the Valley, people could decide whether or not to pick up when you were calling according to where you stood on the totem pole, or how they felt about you at the particular moment you decided to call. It was especially satisfying to less important middle managers to have a visitor in the office and have the telephone gurgle. That way one could either pick up the phone with an excusatory "Sorry, I've gotta take this," to one's visitor, which showed that important people were calling you; or even better, one could cast a glance at the little screen, give a little derogatory flip of the hand, and forward the call by pushing a button. That sent two messages to the visitor. The first was "I'm selective about whom I speak with; not everyone has a claim on my time," and also "You, my friend, are important to me, and not just anyone can interrupt our conversation."

Carmelita also knew, as did all receptionists (they were contracted by the security organization, which gave every one of them a full day of training before they entered upon their duties) a lot more about the phone system. For instance, she knew that phones were tapped at random by Security to see if anyone was making too many personal phone calls (grade levels 3 through 6), or alternatively, passing company confidential information to the competition, or worse, to the press (grade levels 10 and up). She also knew that one vice president at DataDrive was quietly being edged out because of insider trading, an activity revealed to one of Security's contract employees through just such a phone tap. The contract employee, however, had made a big mistake. His big mistake wasn't that he had told his supervisor about the insider trading conversation, because that was what he was supposed to do. The supervisor, who was not a contract employee, but rather was on DataDrive's payroll, knew what to do with such information when it concerned a VP, namely, bury it.

No, the mistake was that because the young security employee was not very technical, he hadn't entirely mastered the mysteries of electronic mail. In trying to transmit the results of his detection to the supervisor, the youth had accidentally included it in a message destined to be sent to every company employee in the Bay area, about safety in the parking lots when you were working late and had to walk a distance to get to your car. The original message had been intended to end with, "Remember, your personal security comes first! Don't hesitate to dial extension 599, and we'll be there in a few minutes to escort you to your vehicle." Now it segued neatly into the following: "Carl, I got a doozey here! Got a VP by the short hairs! Sanford, in Building Twenty. He's been using his cleaning lady, for Christ sake! He gives her all this stuff about end of quarter numbers, tells her to sell short, then he ends up with 'don't forget the upstairs bathroom toilet bowl, 'cause my kid was home from college for the weekend and clogged the damn thing up with toilet paper again.' What do you bet we can get his ass kicked out of here?"

But the young security wiretapper was fated never to know Carl's opinion on that topic. The next morning he found that he had been reassigned to guard duty at the rear gate of a lumberyard in Aptos, which was on the coast and a two hour drive from the apartment he shared with several other young persons who were also just launching their careers. He would have found himself unemployed, but his uncle owned the Bay area franchise of the security company; so he survived—a fact he owed to his mother, who had pleaded for him with her brother. She never told her son anything about this, however, because she didn't want to add to his burden of guilt.

Carmelita knew all these things, of course, because Kurt worked as a bartender at the Silicon Corral, which was a pretty good lunch place by day and a very popular drinking spot for the high tech community at night (all grade levels up to, but not including directors). Kurt was a good bartender, which meant he was a good listener, so he got to know a lot of stuff. Kurt told Carmelita "Any of this stuff I tell you, you keep quiet," and she did, because she loved Kurt and didn't want him to get into trouble. She knew how things got around, as she said to Trudi, who was the only person in the world Carmelita could trust to keep her mouth shut. Trudi had been her floater for almost a year and they were real good friends, at least at work. They almost never saw each other after hours, mostly because Carmelita was either at Kurt's, or at home watching the younger members of her family, and Trudi, of course, had to dash off to her courses three nights a week.

And now Kurt hadn't called in several days, and Carmelita was damned if she was going to call first. Though she was tempted. It was now a little before noon, and he would just be getting out of bed. Carmelita knew that bed well, and not only because she changed its sheets every week. When she had first slept with Kurt at his place, shortly after the first time ever with Kurt (which took place on a beach just above Santa Cruz), she had been appalled by the sour odor that rose to her nostrils as Kurt pulled back the covers. It had been a real turnoff, as she told Trudi later. But of course Kurt was not to be denied, not at that particular moment. So Carmelita had gone along with everything Kurt wanted, which, considering he had only a high school degree, was pretty comprehensive. Carmelita's previous boyfriend had been a math major at

UCSC, and he had lots of creative mathematical ideas about copulation. Carmelita had always associated the intricate positions and deferred resolution of orgasm with the student's interest in mathmatical formulas, so she was surprised to discover that Kurt, though a math illiterate, was himself fairly inventive.

"Though why I have to twist around like a pretzel I'll never know," she confided to Trudi. "It gets them all excited, when I'd really rather just have them hug me for a while, at least to start."

Once Carmelita had taken responsibility for seeing that Kurt had clean bedsheets on a regular basis, she felt better about being pretzelized. At least when her nose was being ground down into the pillow, with Kurt in a peculiar half-standing, half-crouching position behind her, her legs swaying in the air, she no longer suffered nausea from the odor of unwashed sheets. And that was something, as she told Trudi.

Trudi, who would have been willing to chance nausea at least once in exchange for tasting the delights frequently limned to her by her friend, had nodded understandingly. But secretly she had hated herself for being so damned understanding all the time. She would have liked to punch Carmelita at that moment. Though Carmelita was slender and Trudi was not, Trudi felt she had every much a right to be twisted about by a panting boyfriend as Carmelita did. It had just never happened. She had friends, and she went on dates, but that was about it. Maybe, she reflected, the reason was to be found in the fact that Carmelita was Catholic, whereas Trudi, to the extent she was anything, was Lutheran. Exciting things seemed to happen much more frequently to Catholics than to Lutherans.

Carmelita reached for the phone and punched in a number. "I'm calling," she said. "I shouldn't, but what the heck." And at that moment Trudi became aware that a man was standing at the counter of the receptionist's station. Neither she nor Carmelita had heard him come in, though that was no wonder, really, since the doors of Building Fifteen worked silently and the floor was thickly carpeted. Trudi put her knitting down out of sight. You weren't supposed to be knitting, or doing your homework, or talking to your boyfriend on the phone while you were on duty. You were supposed to be alert, and make everyone show their badge and sign in if they were a stranger. And here this guy could have walked right by them!

Trudi shot a quick glance at Carmelita, who had also noticed the man, and had solved the problem by swinging her chair away from him and pretending he was not there. She was talking to Kurt in a low voice. Trudi noticed that the man at the counter appeared to be dancing, or swaying quickly from one foot to another. He was unshaven, and had a mop of unruly black hair. His eyes were crinkly, in a nice way, and he appeared to be maybe thirty-five or so. She stood up.

"Can I help you?" she said.

The man said quickly "Yes. You can tell me where the nearest men's room is."

Trudi thought the man was going to be sick then and there, so she quickly came around from behind the counter and pointed down the corridor. "Down there on the right," she said. "Second door. It's not locked."

The man ran down the hall and pushed open the door of the men's room. Trudi stood open-mouthed. From behind the counter she could hear an invisible Carmelita saying goodbye to Kurt. She slowly returned to her chair. She looked at Carmelita, who looked at her. Finally Carmelita spoke.

"What's gotten into you?" she asked. "You look like you're drunk."

"Oh," said Trudi. "Nothing. Just that guy."

"I don't wanna hear about guys at the moment," said Carmelita sourly. "What guy, anyway?"

"The guy who's in the men's room."

"What *about* him?"

"He's sort of attractive," Trudi said, and she blushed a little. The fact was that the man who was in such a hurry to get to the men's room had reminded her of the leader of the Jackals, a thrash metal group, who had eyed her in a somewhat predatory way the previous Saturday when she had spent an hour at a jazz club in Oakland with four other girls. Except that the men's room man was a little older and much less greasy.

"Don't talk to me about *men*," Carmelita said, putting extra emphasis into the last word. "Men are creeps."

Trudi sensed that something was amiss, and that it must have to do with the phone conversation her friend had just ended. "Is it Kurt?" she asked tentatively.

Carmelita snorted. "I think there was someone there with him. He sounded weird. Like he didn't really want to talk. And too happy, in a way. Kurt's never happy when he wakes up."

Just then the phone gurgled again, and Carmelita picked up the receiver. "Lobby," she said. Then, after a while she said "Hold on, Daph," put her hand over the mouthpiece, and said to Trudi, "Make sure that guy doesn't get away."

"What guy?" said Trudi.

"The guy in the can!" said Carmelita, and she spoke into the phone. "Okay, yeah, he's here. He just came in. He's in the men's room now. Yeah, send her down."

"What was that about?" asked Trudi. "Is he a crook or something?"

"Naw," said Carmelita. She had put the phone down and was reaching for the book of visitors' badges. "He's some big nerd they've been waiting for. HR's sending down a delegation to meet him." HR, of course, was the Human Resources department. "I'm glad he came in when he did. I might have gone off to lunch without telling you."

"He doesn't look much like a nerd," said Trudi. "He looks more like...." She couldn't really find the word that described the man.

"Anyway," said Carmelita, collecting her purse from under the desk, when he comes out of there, *if* he ever comes out, be sure to get a badge on him and sit him down somewhere until Toni or Daphne comes down. They've been waiting for this guy like for weeks now. I heard they're stealing him away from Siegfried Software. He's supposed to be one of those real weird software geniuses. Toni says a guy like that is one in a million. The kind that they pay big money for, only of course, guys like that don't really care about money. Don't know what to do with it."

She stood up and indicated the central drawer of the desk. "There's a Snickers in there, in the back. In case you get hungry." She moved out from the station and started for the door.

"You mean he's like a programmer?" called Trudi after her.

Carmelita turned. "Not a programmer. This guy's what they call a thinker. Sits there for hours or days, doing nothing. Then bingo! he gets an idea that's like far out, wild. Siegfried's gonna be real bummed when they find out we landed him at DataDrive." She shot a glance down the corridor. "Maybe he's sitting now, just waiting for an idea to come out. He sure doesn't seem in a hurry to get on board. I've got to get going. Gotta think how to handle this Kurt situation. Bye, now." And she walked out.

Carmelita hadn't been gone more than a minute or two when the man emerged from the corridor. Trudi, who had picked up her knitting, again shoved it hurriedly out of sight. She smiled at the man.

"Please sign in," she said, indicating the log book. The man looked at her oddly.

"I have to sign in to use the men's room?" he said.

Trudi giggled. "No, of course not. You just have to sign in to get upstairs. And we've already made a badge out for you. The HR people will be here in a minute or so."

The man, whose name was Fenelon, picked up the badge and examined it for a moment. "Arthur Smith," he said.

Trudi felt that for once being a floater had its advantages. She covered four buildings on the DataDrive campus and so she had met more odd computer types than had the typical receptionist.

She knew their strange ways of speech, the detached expressions on their faces as they attempted the activities of daily life. Earrings and ponytails were affected, she knew, by the more normal employees. Trudi had figured out that it was the ones who wore slacks and sleeveless sweaters that were really off the wall. One of these had once taken a fancy to Trudi and would come to the lobby of Building Six just when she was filling in on the first morning break. He would plant himself against the wall and just look at her. After a few mornings of this Trudi had complained to her supervisor, who then had a word with this man's keeper, as Trudi put it to Carmelita. The man ceased coming to stare at Trudi, who missed him and regretted her complaint.

So when the man in the black leather jacket with the elbows out had stared at the badge and said his name as if he'd never heard it before, Trudi was quite tolerant.

"That's you," she said brightly. "Did we spell it right?"

"Why the badge?" asked the man, and this time he turned to look at Trudi. A little gray showed here and there in his mop of wild black hair, and his eyes seemed to bore into Trudi's soul, as she later reported to Carmelita.

Trudi felt her self-confidence ebbing. "The HR people can't take you upstairs unless you're logged in," she said. "And you need the badge, otherwise you might get stopped by someone. This is the lab, you know. They're pretty sensitive about it."

"And why on earth would I want to go upstairs?" said the man, smiling this time.

Trudi found herself getting mad. "Because, Arthur, if you don't you can't join the company, and they can't pay you whatever outrageous sum they've promised you." There! That ought to shut him up.

"This is very funny," said the man.

Trudi said "Look, just sign here and put down the time, and then sit down over there. I'll call HR and find out what's keeping them. You'll find some copies of *UNIX Today*."

The man laughed, and Trudi said "What's so funny?"

"Nothing," he said. "What's your name?"

"Trudi," said Trudi. She felt her cheeks getting red again and hated herself. This guy was old enough to be her father, if her father hadn't waited until he'd made the Golden Circle before marrying Trudi's mom.

"Trudi what?"

But just then from the top of the stairs came the click of heels. It was the delegation from HR.

# two

ONI HUNTER HAD been with HR for several years. She hadn't made director yet, but this was definitely in the cards. Her qualifications were impeccable; she had her A.A., had been trained as a beautician and had run her own salon for three years. During this time she had developed remarkable skills in empathy and communication, both of which are important in the Human Resources field. Then she had suffered some business reverses. One of her girls, a Polish immigrant whose English was terrible but whose own empathic abilities were considerable, had left her and opened Wanda's Hair and Nails just a few blocks away. This was not only inconsiderate—since Toni had always treated Wanda with kindness, making allowances time and again for the fact that she was a foreigner—it was also illegal. Toni had made each of her girls sign an agreement not-to-compete at the time each of them had been engaged. That agreement specified that her employees could not open a competing business within a radius of two miles for a period of two years after they had left Toni. Toni could never be sure, as she reflected on her entrepreneurial days, that it was not this agreement itself that had planted the idea in her girls' cute but normally empty little heads that they could make more money outside of Toni's Place than inside it.

Wanda was the only one who had ventured inside the sacred two-mile circle, however. After consultations with her lawyer, Toni decided not to sue. According to the attorney, who was a graduate of Santa Clara University and therefore knew the terrain, judges did not look favorably on agreements not-to-compete, and Toni might spend a lot of effort pursuing Wanda with little to show for it at the end of the road.

Toni decided to get into a new field. Her then beau, a man named Mark, had a drinking buddy named Judd Trainor who was a recruiter for the high tech industry. Mark talked Toni into meeting Judd, which was a mistake on his part. Judd was immediately taken with her. Toni was really something, as he confided to a sullen Mark a few days later. Her best characteristic, he thought, was her legs, which "went on forever" in Judd's homely phrase. It was true. Toni was willowy, with an enchanting slimness below and an engaging fullness above that just seemed to attract men. She had a beautiful and interesting face. Her eyes were set just a little too far apart, and her lower lip had either been stung by the proverbial bee or was gently set in a permanent pout. Judd had decided right away that he could find a place for Toni in one of the two classy companies on whose behalf he was currently recruiting. Both of these companies were expanding wildly in an orgy of hiring, and needed persons with just Toni's abilities to keep things moving along. Of course he was damned if he was going to tell Toni that. Judd knew human nature well, better even than Toni. He figured he could keep her on the string for six weeks at least, while he investigated possibilities with both the companies and with Toni herself.

As for Toni, she seemed content to put herself literally into Judd's hands. She had a few thousand dollars set aside, and Judd had spoken so highly of her background as being just what would pay off for her in the industry that she was quite sanguine about the future. She would discuss job possibilities with Judd a couple of evenings a week, at first at a small café, and then when the weather turned colder, at Toni's condo in Redwood City. Judd always picked up the tab at the café, and Toni picked up the tab, so to speak, at her condo. Judd never stayed the night, for which Toni was rather grateful, as she never looked her best in the morning. Also, waking up with a man next to her had connotations of permanence that did not appeal to her.

The evening finally came when Judd announced that he had found the right job for Toni. The position was as an HR generalist, he said, with a company called DataDrive. Toni had no idea what HR was, but took Judd's word for it that she would fit right in.

"You're a generalist, you see," he had explained. "Generalists don't have to know anything. They learn on the job. You'll start out administering the benefits program."

"How much does it pay?" Toni had asked. And when she heard the answer she decided to accept the job at once.

"Hold on," said Judd, laughing. "You've got to interview first. But I've got it all set up. I had a word with the hiring manager. He's actually the divisional vice-president for HR, so you'll be starting off at the right level. There's no director of benefit programs yet. If there was you'd be reporting to him. Use the next few months to get in with anyone you can that's a manager. Manage upwards, that's the motto."

That had been four years ago, but Toni had never forgotten Judd's advice. She had applied herself assiduously to learning everything she could. Not about the content of the various jobs she had held, for those could be and were carried out mostly by a succession of admins who had the misfortune to be assigned to work under her, but rather about her bosses and their bosses. Toni spent several hours each week dropping into the office of certain vice-presidents, sometimes to drop a tidbit of news, sometimes to share a merry laugh over an unfortunate employee's peccadillo about which Toni, in her capacity of HR staffer, had privileged knowledge. Toni had a finely developed sense of timing. She always left each vice-president's office a few minutes too early, so that each of these men (there was one woman vice-president, but Toni never sensed a need to share a tidbit with her) wished she had stayed just a moment or so longer.

Toni also had a sense of flair in her attire. She generally wore long skirts, usually with pleats, and blousy shirts. This way her figure was not unduly emphasized. Every so often, though, she showed up at work in one of several clingy knit outfits which did indeed emphasize her figure. The younger vice-presidents were able to store the image of Toni in their neuron banks, and draw upon it at will, which carried them over the long periods during which she was among them in conservative garb. One older VP suffered from short-term memory deficit, however, and while he could recall every detail about his eighth-grade math teacher, Miss Watley, who resembled a genus of amphibian, he couldn't remember a single detail about Toni clasping her arms over her head and stretching upwards toward the ceiling the previous Friday morning, as she related a humorous incident concerning her sister's new dog. All he could remember was that he had tried to commit every detail of the scene to memory. What infuriated him was that he *did* remember the name of the blasted dog. It was Tucker.

The reason Toni didn't come right down to the lobby when she had found out from her admin that Arthur Smith, the software guru, had arrived, was simple. Toni had learned that it was important to put new employees in their place from the getgo. She was well aware how important Arthur Smith would be to the future of research at DataDrive; she had been involved in the recruitment effort from the beginning. Her old friend Judd, whom she saw occasionally, had found out that Smith was on the market. He and Toni had shaped the campaign carefully. Since it was well known in the industry that Smith didn't seem to have any interest in anything that wasn't software, and especially not in women, they decided that Judd would make the approach. Judd knew (from sources he wouldn't reveal) that Smith wanted to move because the development company he worked for had changed the terms of his employment without even consulting him.

"You know what they did?" Judd asked Toni. At the time they were stretched out naked on a white deep pile nylon rug in front of Toni's electric fire. He was feeling quite relaxed, the warmth of the electric fire on his shoulder blades and buttocks inducing a sense of well-being almost equaled by the afterglow of a more than decent mutual orgasm. Five-point-oh on the Richter, as Toni had said. Normally Judd aimed for at least a six-point-five, but they had killed a bottle and a half of Chardonnay which seemed to have dulled Judd's response mechanism.

"What who did?" muttered Toni, who was lying in Judd's shadow and was beginning to feel cold.

"I told you, Siegfried Software, the guys that got Arthur Smith to head their development team. What a bunch of dopes! They pay the guy maybe eighty thousand, no options. The only thing he wanted was the vending machine in the break room had to have Kachina brand blue corn chips with real rancho flavor. Any time, day or night he had to be able to get them. So the dorks change vendors and the new company doesn't carry Kachina. So Smith stops the new VP of R&D in the parking lot one morning—the dork is on his way to work and Smith is on his way to bed—and says if they don't fix the situation in twenty-four hours he's outta there. The VP's had a fight with his wife about something so he's already pissed off, and here's this weirdo, hasn't shaved in five weeks, looks like a bum, stops him in the lot to rant about corn chips! The VP doesn't know him from Adam, 'cause they're never in the building at the same time, so he tells him to fuck off. Smith just smiles at the guy, I heard, never mind from who. Now he's on the market. Biggest fish in the sea!"

Toni had immediately sensed that this was the opportunity she had been waiting for. She was shortly going to be celebrating her thirty-seventh birthday, and she wanted desperately to get the director slot for corporate recruiting. Time was running out for her. High tech was a young person's environment, and she just couldn't go on being an individual contributor forever. The day would come when the VPs wouldn't look forward to her little visits, her silvery laugh, with quite as much eagerness as they did now. As a director, she would have status that didn't depend on her smile, her body, her little jokes.She could exercise some real power in the group vice-president's Monday afternoon staff meeting. Often the divisional VP for Human Resources didn't care to attend these meetings, and so from time to time, as often as he dared, he arranged to be out of town. Toni would sit in for him. She knew the divisional vice-president was having a hard time at home, because one of her few friends happened to be his admin, and sometimes caught a fragment of a phone conversation. Men having a hard time at home were Toni's specialty. Not that she offered them more than a sympathetic ear. She wasn't completely devoid of sense, and was careful never to do anything that smacked of coming on to any of the execs. How they might interpret the tone of voice she used when addressing them, or the little smiling faces she put on resumes she thought deserved their special attention, was none of her affair.

The very next morning she had happened to pass Sammi Boyadjian's office just as he was entering it. Sammi was the group VP and he also sat on ExCom. They almost collided in the hall. It was early and there was no one else about.

"Sammi, if you've got a minute..." said Toni. "Something I found out from a friend."

Sammi had immediately invited Toni into his office. She sat on the edge of his conference table and told him about Arthur Smith. She omitted the details about the blue corn chips; that knowledge would be her little ace in the hole.

"You mean you think we can get this guy?" said Sammi. "Would Jerzy and him get along?" Sammi was from Brooklyn and disdained niceties of syntax. But his question was very *apropos.* Jerzy was the VP for product development and was generally known to be a madman.

"I can handle Jerzy," said Toni.

"I dunno," said Sammi morosely. "We been having a lot of trouble with Jerzy. He comes on board, what is it, a year, eighteen months ago? Bingo! He fires five managers just like that. Jeez, next thing I know he's got a bunch of reqs floating around out there, has to rebuild the whole staff."

"I remember," Toni said soothingly. But Sammi was on the warpath.

"I ask him before staff, hey Jerzy, what's going on here? I mean five guys, just like that! I get their wives calling Eleanor, crying, saying has Sammi lost control or what? I mean calling my wife, for God's sake! I don't want people bothering her already. I get onto Jerzy's case, he says 'I gotta start out knocking heads together so the rest'll know who's boss. They'll all work a lot harder now,' he says, for God's sake. I mean the guy's got the sympathy of a Turk, you know what I mean? 'The rest'll work a lot harder.' The guy's a nut case! Half the senior engineers turned over within a year!"

Toni knew that Jerzy wasn't really a nut case. He was simply an honest sadist, that was all. But for the moment it was important to soothe Sammi's nerves, and this she did.

"Jerzy will get along fine with Arthur Smith," she said. "Because if he doesn't, you'll fire his ass out of here. And you don't have to tell him that. I will. I'll fire him, too, if it comes to that."

Sammi looked at Toni with wonder. This was a woman! "Toni," he said, "you're a tower of strength. A freakin' tower of strength." He pronounced it "strenth," which had always irritated Toni, who had not been to Brooklyn, nor ever even looked over at it from Manhattan. But this morning she felt quite tolerant of Sammi.

"You're going to have Arthur Smith working for you within a week," she said, smiling. "I guarantee it. You just get Tookie to fire up the PR staff for an announcement."

In the event it had taken more than a week to land Arthur Smith.

Judd had picked that very evening to decide to take a few days off and drive down to the Four Corners. He had recently decided that he was partly of Native American heritage, based on a comment made a while back by a go-go dancer at the Leather Strip, a bar tucked away in the wilderness between Alviso and Milpitas. The dancer, whose name was Tiffany, was half Apache herself, if she could be believed, and therefore had keen eyesight. She could (she told Judd) recognize one of her own kind a mile away. So it was no great feat for her to pick Judd out from among all the other men standing at the bar, even though smoking was allowed at the Leather Strip, so that the air was thick and hazy. As soon as Tiffany had finished her number and had been lowered from her cage, she tugged on a half T-shirt that was just a little bit too tight for her and made straight for Judd. He was partly flattered and partly embarrassed. The embarrassment came from the fact that he was squiring a group of Japanese businessmen who represented investors planning to open a factory in San Jose. The factory would take advantage of the cheap labor available in the East Bay area that in turn was a consequence of a few years of layoffs of tens of thousands of relatively well-qualified engineers and production personnel.

His guests from the Orient were enchanted with Tiffany. For someone who was half Apache she had the most amazing head of platinum-blonde hair. Of the six or seven Japanese only one could speak English reasonably well, and his services as an interpreter were immediately at a premium among his colleagues. The man from MITI insisted on presenting her with a diamond watch which he had purchased just that afternoon at an exclusive jewelry shop in the Stanford Shopping Center. The watch had been intended for his mistress in the Akoyama district of Tokyo, but the man from MITI, who had never studied Latin (and indeed, ignored the existence of the language) nonetheless obeyed the principle of *carpe diem* and presented the tiny white box to Tiffany with a little bow.

Tiffany had been working the circuit, as she later put it to Judd, for a few years and so was already familiar with the largesse of senior Japanese executives. She assumed that what was in the box was a pin of some kind. So when she finally opened it to the encouraging cries of the surrounding crowd, which had swollen now to include not only the seven Japanese and Judd, but an assortment of grinning accountants, sales managers, truck drivers, and one or two sullen women, she was first flabbergasted and then aghast. Tiffany knew real diamonds when she saw them, and though she had she had never studied French, she knew the meaning of the word Piaget.

It must be said, to her credit, that she made an attempt to return the timepiece to the man from MITI. When he refused with a grin and put his arm around her waist, moving his hand up toward the frayed bottom of the half T-shirt, Tiffany turned her pretty head and gave Bob, the bartender, a little look. The next thing that happened was that a large young gentleman in gray slacks and a blue sports jacket materialized at her side and insinuated himself smoothly between Tiffany and the man from MITI, who perforce removed his arm from her waist. Tiffany was hustled to the rear of the bar and through a door labelled "Staff Only." There she whispered into the right ear of the young man, who disappeared once more into the bar, returning in a minute with a somewhat disheveled Judd in tow. As soon as he realized what had happened, Judd was just as pleased to leave the scene, as he had sensed from early on that the man from MITI, in the calm of the following day, must inevitably come to regret his generous impulse with regard to the Piaget, and might have tried to enlist Judd's help in recovering it. Judd was not about to take on that task. Not with a half-breed Apache like Tiffany. He preferred by far to maintain and perhaps even to improve relations in that department. All in all, he felt it might be just as well to write off the Japanese contract.

So that was how Judd, with Tiffany's assistance, came to be seeking his roots in the great American Southwest at the precise moment Toni needed his assistance in devising a snare, baited with

Kachina brand blue corn chips with real rancho flavor, for Arthur Smith.

After a few days Judd returned from the Four Corners with Tiffany. He deposited her at the Milpitas town house she shared with her girl friend and made tracks for his own place in Mountain View, where he found his answering machine bulging with messages and threats from Toni, as well as one fairly lengthy disquisition from someone who sounded like a very disturbed Japanese with but a limited command of English. Judd could make neither head nor tail of this message and promptly deleted it along with most of Toni's. He saved one or two of the latter, for their unique and piquant phraseology.

THE PLAN THEY eventually cooked up was simplicity itself. Judd did some basic research. Among other things, he found out where Arthur Smith lived. Judd drove over there one morning around six and camped out until Arthur showed up on his battered Peugeot bicycle. Arthur was blonde and rather plump, for all that he rode a bicycle. He proved surprisingly amenable to Judd's proposition, which was that Arthur leave Siegfried Software and move into a special two-room office which was even now being set up for him in Building Fifteen at DataDrive. One room of the office would have a desk with three of the industry's most powerful machines on it; a conference table, a dartboard with a photo of Bill Gates mounted in the center and a holder with fifteen balanced English darts, and a selection of colored wood yoyos. There would be no telephone, since (as Judd had learned) Arthur detested being interrupted by gurgles while he was thinking. Instead, the admin down the hall would screen every call and would slip notes to Arthur through a special sort of mail slot which Facilities had cut into the door. Arthur could collect these from time to time. Or he could leave them lay there, as Judd put it.

In the chamber adjoining the main office the facilities staff was installing two vending machines. The first was being re-engineered

to accommodate the oddly sized plastic bottles of a popular fruit
drink. The second machine would be dedicated exclusively to
Kachina brand blue corn chips. Seven of the eight ranks would
have the real rancho flavor; the eighth would have an assortment.
There were also a bongo board, a personalized bike rack and a
futon rolled up against the wall for those moments when Arthur
might feel in need of relaxation.

"The assortment of chips will be for just in case," said Judd to
Arthur. "In my experience you never know when things might
indicate a change. You might want to stick with real rancho flavor
forever. Or you might not." They were by this time sitting on the
cushions scattered about the linoleum floor of Arthur's living
room. His apartment was a unit in a nondescript block of wooden
flats that reminded Judd, as he later said to Toni, of early Okie
chicken coops.

Arthur had nodded in agreement. The mixing of other flavors in
the eighth rank had proved a master stroke. Money was not even
mentioned. And that was that. It was agreed that Arthur would
report to Building Fifteen at noon the following Monday to sign
on. Noon was what Judd had agreed to with Toni, who wanted to
announce Arthur's signing-on to Sammi Boyadjian just before his
Monday staff, which would go into session at one o'clock.

Unfortunately, Judd's research on Arthur Smith's likes and dis-
likes had been carried out so swiftly, under Toni's harsh urging,
that he had not been able to plumb very deeply into Arthur's soul.
Arthur had a soul—though to look at him you might not have
thought so. And in his soul burned a passionate love for his
mother, Felicia Shadroe, who was a well-known conservative
columnist who wrote polemics against democrats and abortionists
from her luxury apartment in Aspen. Arthur felt that his mother
ought to share in the good news that he was leaving the uncaring
folks at Siegfried, and because he detested the phone he decided to
pay her a visit. It was about twelve hundred miles to Aspen, and
Arthur figured he could do this distance on his Peugeot bicycle in a

couple of weeks. This schedule, of course, clashed somewhat with his commitment to Judd, but Arthur knew from experience that little importance would be attached to his showing up a few days late. He was aware that his talent didn't grow on trees, as his mother used to boast when he was little. DataDrive would wait. Besides, Arthur doubted that the offices would be ready by the following Monday anyway. After Judd left him he went into his apartment and standing in front of the fridge, he drank a pint of orange juice. Then he washed his face and hands carefully, brushed his teeth, removed his shoes and tan slacks, turned on Good Morning America and fell into a deep slumber.

# three

DEAR EMILE,

     *The most amazing thing has happened to me! I am employed, well and truly. For the last week I've been ensconced in my new offices. That's offices, as in plural. I have two rooms, one of which appears to have been some kind of lunch room in the past. It's got a couple of vending machines standing in it at the moment, but I'm going to have them removed pretty soon. For the moment I'm leaving them there, because (a) no one else seems to know they are there and (b) you don't need money to work them! I'm not joking. You push the little buttons and down drops the item, with no coin of the realm needed. There isn't much of a selection, though.*

    *My regular office has a bunch of computers. They're on my desk, which is immense. It runs along two of the four walls. I have no idea how these computers work, nor what it is I'm supposed to do with them. They seem to be turned on all the time, because they emit a gentle humming noise, but I can't get anything to show up on the screen. Nor can I turn them off. It's a tremendous waste of energy, of course, but what the heck!*

    *But let me begin from the beginning. You remember the morning I left Terre Haute. I was feeling pretty low for a while—first because* we've been such good friends, and second, well, frankly, I may have had one too many sips of that delightful Armagnac. In fact, I had a good cry shortly after crossing the Illinois line. You know, I think it was a delayed reaction to everything that happened. Not only not getting tenure, but also Antje's leaving me. It seems funny, but I think I never got all that stuff out of my system even though it was almost a year ago.

The thing that precipitated the tears I think—(how can we ever know these things for sure?) was my thinking about those faculty meetings way back when I first started teaching. Why that should have popped into my head I have no idea. We never seemed to be able to address any of the important issues, like how the budgeteers were clamping down on the money for the humanities, and diverting it all to the engineering and science departments. It seems as if the only thing we ever discussed was how to allocate the covered parking spaces in the faculty garage. Where I was allowed to park my eight-year old Chevrolet was a mark of greater social standing than course evaluations or publications. At my very first faculty meeting I tried to introduce a modicum of rational discourse on this issue, but my words were swept away by a tide of emotion. For the remainder of my time at the college I trudged in every morning from the farthest reaches of the parking lot, through snow, mud and dust. Not that I cared, as I've told you many times.

Anyway, for some reason I just started sobbing. But after a while I started feeling better.

It was an uneventful trip, for the most part. My car held together remarkably well. I had a problem with overheating in Colorado, but a friendly mechanic diagnosed the problem as a dirty radiator and flushed it out. After that it was as good as new. No problems of any kind.

One thing I didn't count on was how much gas it would take to get out here. I panicked a little crossing the Great Salt Desert, because I only had about 50 dollars left. No matter how I did the math I couldn't see how I could make it to the coast. I ended up getting a job

at a diner in a town called Winnemucca, Nevada. A tiny place, with
wonderful people. They say "hello" to you on the street! I worked there
for about five weeks, and believe me I considered staying, though there
isn't anything like a coastline there. Nor was there much interest in
French literature, even Camus. I slept in the car (I can see your reaction!) except for two nights toward the end that I spent with the relief
cook. She is a housewife in her everyday life, but Norma (the regular
cook) got such a bad case of the flu that Joey (that's the owner of the
place) was afraid she'd either scare off or infect all the customers. So he
got Mickie in to take over. Mickie was not a bad cook, and she was
quite good-looking. Resembled a younger Cher. She was about thirty-
four or -five, and her husband was some kind of farmer, or rancher.
Oh, yes, there was a husband. Except he was off buying cow feed or
something. When Mickie found out I was sleeping in the car she invited me home, but not until her husband was out of the way for a couple of days.

When I left Winnemucca I had managed to put away about 800
dollars. This is a great country! Of course, I didn't have any food
expenses; the diner provided everything in that respect. So I was doing
OK when I got to California and crossed the Central Valley. There are
lots of valleys here: Central, Death, Silicon. I had come out of the
Central Valley and was intending to pass south of the Silicon, heading
for the coast, when, fiddling with the radio dial, I managed to lock
into NPR. What do I get but a program on middle-aged men and
their medical problems! A call-in show, no less. There was a panel of
three experts—two doctors, and a woman psychologist who apparently specializes in the field. At the time I was passing through the
strangest place you ever saw—a sort of little pass in some hills, where
everything is brown and yellow. I guess they rarely get rain out this
way. But the colors weren't what made it so strange. The hills were
covered by hundreds, no, thousands of windmills! Not the Dutch kind
with a little house, but the kind we've got out in the country at home
that are used for pumping water. And most of these things were

whirling around wildly. The funny thing is, there were no pipes! Not a one. I couldn't figure that one out.

Well, as soon as I got out of the hills I decided I'd call into the talk show program. You didn't have to give your name. It had been a while since I'd even thought about my health, and maybe I felt a bit guilty for having neglected the subject. I pulled over at a phone booth outside a Chinese restaurant in the next town and called the station. I'm afraid I used your credit card number, as I couldn't find enough change to pay for the whole call. That's why I've included five dollars with this letter. I got through to the program with no delay and asked about whether there was any progress being made toward effective treatment for the prostate, in case it should decide to get out of whack. You recall, no doubt, that I used to be obsessed with that sort of thing.

I got back in the car and drove along, checking the map from time to time and listening to what turned out to be a very lively discussion around my question. Of course, I knew there wasn't any settled medical opinion. I just thought it would be a good topic for the panel to sink their teeth into, so to speak, and I was right.

It's possible that I took a wrong turn or two, because instead of heading for the coast I found myself going north toward San Francisco on California 101, which is a horrid excuse for a highway. But I had gotten so involved in the discussion on the radio that I just didn't notice where I was going. And then I had this violent urge to void my bladder. It hit me quite suddenly. There was no place to do it along the highway, except of course I could have pulled off the road and done it facing away from traffic, partially shielded by my car. But at the rate the cars were passing I figured that maybe five hundred people would have had a chance to see me. So instead I took a chance and pulled off at the next exit. That's what an Indiana middle class upbringing does to you, I guess.

I hoped to find a restaurant or just a clump of trees on a quiet side street. Emile, it was awful! I found myself in a labyrinth of streets, lined with faceless buildings of the very modern sort—the kind with-

*out windows or doors. At least that's how it appeared at the time. There were signs everywhere giving the names of the companies whose buildings they were, but all I wanted was a sign saying "Men."*

*The situation was worse than desperate. I stopped the car and asked a friendly Asian youth wearing some kind of badge around his neck where I could find the door of the building he had apparently just emerged from. Well, it was right in front of me! He must have thought I was mad! His English was remarkably free of accent, by the way. Must have been in this country a long time.*

*I rushed into the lobby of the building. By that time I was about ready to pee into the potted palms. A young girl at the front desk pointed out the men's room and I just made it. I mean, just!* De justesse! *What a relief!*

*It took me quite a while to recover. After I had composed myself I came out. And then things got really interesting....*

# four

TONI FIGURED SHE had waited long enough. She checked herself in the mirror in the ladies room. Not that she particularly gave a damn about whether Arthur Smith found her attractive, or professional, or whatever. He might be a fantastic developer, but he was still just a nerd, as far as she was concerned. The computer industry might be propelled along its course by the combined efforts of thousands of nerds like Arthur, but those who set the course, who stood on the bridge and made the decisions that affected those thousands, they were not nerds. They were men of power, and though Toni was still a mere lieutenant in the official hierarchy, she knew well that the captains and admirals had their favorites. She had attained that status and she intended to keep it. And one way to keep it was always to look her best when strolling the decks, or going up and down the gangplank.

When she got to the bottom of the stairs and looked around the lobby she was first confused, and then irritated. She stalked over to the receptionist's station. Trudi's yarn had become entangled in a stapler, and she was bent over, trying to disengage it. Trudi started nervously as she looked up to see Toni looming over the counter. It was too late to hide the knitting bag, so she just gave a little smile.

"Where is he?" said Toni. "Assuming he hasn't just walked on into the labs," she added drily, glancing at the mass of yarn.

Trudi stood up and pointed. "He's over there," she said, indicating Fenelon, who had retreated to the Danish modern sofa that defined the waiting area of the lobby.

Toni stared and then looked back at Trudi. "You're sure that's him? That man doesn't look like a software genius."

Trudi smirked slightly and indicated the sign-in sheet. "There he is," she said. "Arthur Smith."

Toni composed herself and looked again across the lobby. Arthur Smith wore a tattered black leather jacket and faded jeans. He had a shaggy mop of blue-black hair, and a lean, pale, bearded face. A yellow scarf dangled around his neck. He looked like a refugee from North Beach, Toni thought to herself. Like a poet who ought to be frequenting cheap cafes. Even from where she stood she could see that he was lean, even bony, whereas all the software geniuses Toni was aware of had a certain soft podginess about them that bespoke too much junk food and a general lack of fresh air, sunlight and exercise. Arthur's skin was pale, she saw, but it was somehow a healthy pale, perhaps caused by too much thought, or worry about some personal matter. Since one of HR's missions was to see after the well-being of the employees of the company, it was well within the scope of her job to find out just what was gnawing at Arthur's mind, and she would certainly do so at the right moment.

Finally she saw that he had become aware that she was there. She put on a bright smile and crossed to him, holding out her hand.

"You're Arthur Smith?" she asked.

Fenelon smiled back, stood up, and took her hand in his. Her hand was warm. He said nothing. He could see that this woman, whoever she was, seem a little disconcerted by his silence. She was pretty attractive, but she seemed to have a no-nonsense manner about her. A still, small voice warned him not to trust her, nor say too much.

"I'm Toni Hunter," said the woman. "I'm in charge of the Human Resources department for this division of DataDrive, at least so far as recruiting is concerned. We are very glad to see you. Please come up to my office. There's a little paperwork I need you to fill out."

As Fenelon went up the stairs he remembered the old story by Mark Twain he had read in his youth. It was *The Prince and the Pauper.* In it a young boy from the London slums changes places with another boy who is the crown prince of England. Each lives the other's life for a while. Fenelon was aware that there must inevitably be a dénouement to the adventure that appeared to be unfolding before him, just as there was in the Twain story. But for the present, he thought, I'll let myself be swept along. It'll probably end in a few minutes.

As Fenelon followed Toni down the corridor on the second floor he was able to look over a partition into a series of small enclosures that resembled pens. These were apparently the workplaces of the employees who must now be having lunch. Fenelon was able to glimpse the evidence of personal lives; photomontages tacked onto little bulletin boards, more photos, mostly of small children, taped to the sides of computer screens, a few humble potted plants, mostly diminutive cacti. Each cubicle had a desk, a telephone, a computer and one or more filing cabinets. At the college Fenelon had shared with a colleague an office that had walls and a door that closed, and which boasted lots of wood—wood in the desks and chairs and tables, wood paneling on the walls, wood in the window frames and in the door. Here, on the second floor of this building belonging to some company whose name Fenelon, for the life of him, couldn't recall, there was no wood at all. Unless you counted the cacti, he reflected.

In Toni's office he sat at a little round conference table while she gathered some papers from her desk. Then she sat down at the table herself, not across from him, but next to him, spreading the papers out, and then sitting back and crossing her legs.

"We've just got to get you through the routine," she said, again smiling at him. Fenelon was acutely aware of how much he wanted to look down and to his right, to see just how far her skirt might have ridden up on her thighs. "First, we've got the most important one—the offer letter. Please read it carefully and countersign it at the bottom."

Fenelon took the paper she had given him. It was an offer of employment to Arthur Smith from DataDrive, Inc. Yes, that was the name of the company. Fenelon recalled it now; it had been on the little sign outside the building and it was on the badge he was wearing. He read the letter. Then he read it again.

He couldn't believe his eyes. This company was proposing to engage Arthur Smith at a salary of one hundred fifty thousand dollars a year. In addition Arthur would be granted options for thirty thousand shares of stock at a price of fourteen dollars per share, the options to become vested over the next five years. The last paragraph of the letter dealt with what appeared to be an issue of food. It mentioned something about fruit juices and diet drinks, and blue corn chips, whatever they were. Fenelon didn't bother to reread this part.

"You want me to sign this?" he asked Toni. She smiled at him.

"For openers," she said.

Fenelon had been a Cub Scout for three years, and a Boy Scout for five, in a town where Scouting was taken seriously. He had earned many merit badges, and could still recite the Scout oath verbatim. He felt strongly that by signing the letter he would be headed down the path of damnation. To sign as Arthur Smith would be an act of which his den mother would not have been proud.

On the other hand, since leaving Terre Haute he had already committed himself to the road less traveled, so to speak. Why not see where it led?

Toni was looking at him, with just a hint of a frown. "Is there anything in the offer that you don't like?" she asked. "Judd, that is,

Mr. Trainor, told me he had discussed everything with you." This was, of course, not entirely the truth. Judd had told Toni that money and options had not been discussed at all. But he had advised her to make it a generous offer, although the only thing that Arthur was likely to be concerned with would be the availability of his favorite snack.

"No," said Fenelon. "It's just fine." And he signed "Arthur Smith" in a bold, flowing script with the ballpoint pen Toni had put in front of him.

There were other papers. Fenelon had to swear that he was not bringing any proprietary data with him from Siegfried Software, which was easy to do since he had never even heard of that particular company. In fact it wasn't until they got to the withholding forms that Fenelon again had some doubts about the course of action he was taking.

Fortunately, by now it was after one o'clock. Toni stood up and said "Now, Arthur, I have to rush to a meeting. I'm going to leave you in the capable hands of my administrator, Daphne. We call her Daph for short. She'll help you finish up and then she'll show you to your new office." And Toni went off to announce the proud acquisition of Arthur Smith to Sammi's Monday afternoon staff meeting.

Daphne was indeed helpful in one important respect. Fenelon had no idea what Arthur Smith's Social Security number was. And since this was the first felony he had ever committed, if indeed it was a felony and not merely something that was happening to him, he really had no idea whether it would be better to put down his own Social Security number, or try to guess at Arthur's. The likelihood of guessing correctly would be about the same of his winning the Indiana lottery, he realized. And a math colleague of his at the college had once told him that he was sixty times more likely to be struck by lightning in the next year as he was to win the lottery. Fenelon had been impressed by this comparison and had repeated it to one of his students who bought five lottery tickets religiously every week. "Getting struck by lightning sucks," was her comment.

His present dilemma was solved by Daphne who, seeing him hesitate, said "I know what's happening to you! You don't remember your own Social Security number! But it so happens that I know it already!" And seeing the shock in Fenelon's eyes she added helpfully "Don't worry, it's not a sign of senility. Lots of people don't know their number. In fact, in software we get people who don't know their home telephone number! Right after Mr. Trainor met with you last week he called and gave me all your details. And speaking of phones, I even know you don't have a telephone at home! And that you hate cars and only ride your bike. He said you keep all your important personal papers in a folder in your refrigerator. Is that really true?"

"Oh yes," said Fenelon. "It's true. It's the only free space left in my house."

"I thought you lived in an apartment," said Daphne. "That's what Mr. Trainor told us. Apartment 105, in the Oakfest Complex in Sunnyvale."

"Well, yes," said Fenelon. "But I call it my house. Because I'd like to have a house someday."

"Well, with this package you'll be able to afford one," said Daphne, with a note of envy. "Even in Silicon Valley."

"Have you ever been to Death Valley?" Fenelon asked. He was thinking that Death Valley sounded like the sort of isolated spot he might use as a refuge when the *merde* hit the fan.

"Never," said Daphne. "I share a house in Tahoe. That's the only place I ever go."

"Tahoe? Where's that?"

Daphne looked at him in wonder. Finally she shook her head a little and said, "It's really true about you software gurus!"

Fenelon had no idea what she meant by that. But he seemed to be almost finished with the formalities of joining DataDrive. Daphne stood up and he did likewise, following her through the door of Toni's office and back down the corridor. Now all the little pens were filled with activity. He could hear the murmur of voices on telephones. Perhaps one of these murmuring voices was speaking with the receptionist in the lobby, who was frantically calling upstairs to inform someone—anyone—that the real Arthur Smith had appeared, and that the man who had just signed up with DataDrive at five times the salary he had received as an assistant professor of French language and literature, a subject in which he had a Ph.D., was nothing more nor less than an imposter. Fenelon descended the stairs to the lobby behind Daphne. He walked across the lobby and was just following Daphne through the door when he heard a loud, deep male voice calling to him.

"Hey, buddy!"

Fenelon's heart rose into his throat. This was it. At least he had not actually taken any of this company's money. The whole thing could be passed off as a joke. He turned. There, leaning against the receptionist's counter, was a man in uniform. He had some kind of radio strapped like a gun to his waist, and he was jangling a bunch of keys. Fenelon tried to talk but nothing came out of his throat but a little air.

"Sorry, but you'll have to give up that badge," said the man. "It's only good for this building anyway. Visitors keep walking away with them and the receptionists catch heck for it. Don't they, Carmelita?" and he peered behind the counter at the invisible receptionist.

Daphne had reentered the building and unpinned the badge from Fenelon's lapel. "My fault," she said brightly. "I forgot. I'll show you where you'll be working as soon as I take you to get your permanent badge. Here, Frank," and she tossed the badge across the lobby to the man. "See ya later." And she smiled at Fenelon, who followed her through the door and into the bright sunshine of a Silicon Valley summer afternoon.

# five

JERZY BOBOCHEK, VICE-PRESIDENT for software development, wasn't an enlightened manager. He simply didn't believe in all this crap about togetherness and team-building, and all the other horseshit that HR was always clogging up the E-mail with. Jerzy had been graduated from a fairly second-rate technical institute in the Southeastern part of the United States, but there was nothing second-rate about his mind, which was like a steel trap, as he often told his colleagues. Of course, he had used the phrase jokingly, with plenty of quotation marks surrounding it. Though he was not acquainted with the word fatuous, he nevertheless did not wish to appear so. Hence the quotation marks.

Jerzy knew quite a bit about software development, but even more about human nature. In particular, he knew how fearful most of the engineers were who worked the intellectual fields under his watchful overseer's eye. He had developed a marvelous method of getting his boys and girls, as he called them, to toe the line. This was simply to reassign bodies from one project to another, and periodically to cancel projects at random. Jerzy was perfectly aware that many of the investments in these projects wouldn't pay off in any case, and he also was aware that the company couldn't afford to continue all the projects his department had accepted. Once a project was canceled those who had been toiling at it were given two months to find another assignment. Since cancellations and the creation of new projects were not synchronized, those unfortunates who had kept their noses to the grindstone and who had failed to devote at least fifty percent of their time to politicking with the managers of projects that might have a better chance of surviving, endured several weeks of terror before undergoing something called "outprocessing."

Jerzy was always solicitous of these men and women, particularly those few who were in their forties or even older. He knew how difficult it would be for them to find alternative employment. It was a young person's world, after all.

When Jerzy had fired five of his direct reports within two months of his joining DataDrive, he had been surprised when his wife had received calls from the wives of these ex-managers. He hadn't realized until then how soft things had been at DataDrive. The idea that these former employees hadn't been able to take their dismissals like men, but instead had gone whining to their wives, made him sick for the future of the country. The thought that his own wife could have had any influence on his decision was, of course, ludicrous. Jerzy was paid to make tough decisions, as he often told his wife, whose name was Lisa, and who was successor to Jerzy's first wife Betty. Lisa was young, indeed very young, and both worshipped and was a little afraid of Jerzy. She drove a BMW convertible and had charge cards for Nordstrom's and Macy's, as well as a gold Visa card in her own name. Lisa had struggled with the firing situation, which Jerzy finally had resolved by getting them an unlisted phone number.

Jerzy didn't have many friends at work. For one thing, he was ultraconservative, and although most Silicon Valley employees tended to vote Republican, that was mostly due to youthful optimism and the fact that they were still employed. It did not mean that they tolerated fascism.

Jerzy belonged, in fact, to a right-wing group called Firebrands of Freedom. This group had been founded in the far-off McCarthy era by a former member of the Croatian fascist organization called the Ustashi. This gentleman had fled to the USA from Eastern Europe, after the second world war and after setting a new record for individually-inflicted civilian deaths. The figure was two hundred thirty-one, not counting children under fifteen. The founder had been one of the earliest postwar figures to spot the Red Menace, and had therefore had many friends in powerful places in Washington. He had passed away by the time Jerzy was graduated from the second-rate technical institute, but the baton had been passed to others who espoused his philosophy of "Shoot First."

Though Jerzy didn't have many friends, he did get a lot of respect. For one thing, he met all his MBOs. MBO stood for management by objectives, one of a number of theoretical approaches to management in the Valley. So using it to mean "objectives" didn't really make much sense if you took time to think about it, which no one did. Each executive at DataDrive was assigned MBOs, to be attained by the end of the following quarter. Everything at DataDrive, as indeed in the rest of the Valley, was driven by quarterly goals, whether this made any sense or not.

Where Jerzy really excelled was in cutting costs. This he did by cutting projects. Of course, merely cutting projects wouldn't mean anything at all if the only thing that came out of it was more new projects. So much depended on how these things were entered on the books. If one accepted too many projects for the resources at one's disposal, one gained much credit for making superhuman efforts. If one canceled projects because they were finally revealed to reflect the mistaken assumptions, goals or egos of other managers (the ones who had dreamed them up and foisted them on Jerzy's department), then one gained credit for coming in under budget for the quarter.

Jerzy had worked this all out. The most important projects of all were those of political importance, because they had the attention of ExCom, and in one or two cases, the Board of Directors. These would not be allowed to fail. There were only a few of these, but they received a lot of Jerzy's time. They were not necessarily staffed with the very best talent of the department. Jerzy had long ago realized that the very best people had an unfortunate tendency toward independence and might not be willing to take the strain that a superhuman effort required. So the best minds of the department were set to work on projects that were of technical, but not political, importance. Project Nemo was the most notable example. One of his top boys, an Indian named Chatterjee, was running that one.

Those working on tough technical projects were not pushed hard. Jerzy knew enough about the working of the technical mind to know that the best people pushed themselves, though occasionally taking time out for play. And when he found it desirable to cancel a project that had involved some of his top performers, he also knew enough to look the other way. Jerzy knew that at least one of his people was presently working on a screen play about a series of mysterious murders in a Pacific Northwest logging town. At least two others were developing computer games. And one was involved on the Internet in an exciting chess tournament, whose other participants included a computer scientist from CERN, in Geneva, Switzerland; two programmers from the Russian Academy of Science; a minor official of the Ministry of Finance in Belarus; and a janitor who nightly swept the offices of a high tech company in Melbourne, Australia. None of this bothered Jerzy, so long as the good people stayed around. You never knew when you might suddenly need them.

Jerzy did have one good friend at DataDrive. This was the director of hardware sales for the U.S. His name was Salamon, but because he was just a bit exophthalmic and adenoidal to boot, and because these conditions made him resemble a fish, people tended to call him Salmon. His mother had named him King, probably in a hopeful reference to the wise Biblical monarch. As it was, he was

known as King Salmon by everyone who was not engaged at the
moment in addressing him to his face.

King and Jerzy met every Tuesday for a couple of hours at
Woggly's, which was a bar in Mountain View located down an alley
off Castro Street. There they would get stinko on Black Russians.
King lived not far away and could stagger home on his own.
Tuesday was Lisa's bridge night, and so Jerzy could count on being
picked up. Thus neither would run the risk of being stopped by the
police for a DUI. At Woggly's each would share details of his managerial existence of the previous week. Since Jerzy was in software
and King in hardware there was no rivalry present, at least not in
the stab-you-in-the-back-oops-sorry-Charlie way that existed in
every large company in Silicon Valley. Instead there was a friendly
sort of banter, in which each would exchange anecdotes for the edi-
fication of the other, illustrating what advancement each had made
in managerial science.

Jerzy would sometimes share these anecdotes with Lisa on the
way home. King's exploits were just too good to keep to himself.
For example, a few weeks ago he had heard a really good one.

"You know what this guy, the King Salmon, did last week?" he
chuckled, as Lisa wheeled the BMW toward Los Altos Hills. "See,
he's got this PR group reporting to him, and the top person in it,
she's really good at her job, well she decides to leave the company.
So they've got a headcount, right? It's been open for a couple of
months. And the number two person, he's a guy who really wants
the slot. But he's kind of shy, you know, scared of the King. So it
takes him a while to work up his courage. In the meantime he's
busting his ass, doing two jobs, his own and this dame's."

Lisa winced a little when she heard Jerzy use the word "ass." She
didn't like swearing. She hoped that she and Jerzy would have a
child some day, and she wanted the baby to grow up in the right
atmosphere.

"So," Jerzy went on, "finally he gets brave and a few days ago he
goes into King's office and says he'd like to apply for the job. Thinks

he could really make something out of it. So King looks him in the eye and says, 'well, what do you think the job ought to be?' See, the job's open, but it hasn't yet been advertised on E-mail.

"So this poor schmuck, he goes home and he works and works on a plan on how he'd do the job, all the possibilities, how it would expand the business, a whole action plan, maybe ten pages. Real good stuff. So he leaves it on King's desk last Friday." At this point Jerzy could no longer control himself and started to laugh. After a bit he quieted down and continued.

"So Monday, yesterday, this guy goes into King's office bright and early. King is there of course. And the guy says 'Well, what did you think of my plan?' And King looks him in the eye and he says 'Great, it's a great plan. It clearly calls for someone with at least eight years' experience, and certainly an MBA. So I'm afraid you don't qualify.' Imagine! He gets the guy to do his job specs for him, also the plan on how to upgrade the whole group, and then tells the guy the work he did is so good he's done himself out of the job! Oh, that's a good one!"

Lisa appeared bothered by this story. "I think that's just cruel," she said.

"That's the point, baby," said Jerzy. "Life in business is cruel. It's mean and cruel. God, I hope you never have to get involved in it." And he placed his hand firmly on her thigh as they turned into his driveway.

THAT HAD BEEN a little while ago. This particular Tuesday night, Jerzy sought King's advice. "You're the master," he began. Which was the right way to begin with the King, who had achieved a perfect score on the Graduate Record Exam and still let everyone know about it ten years later, and who had two master's degrees, an MBA and an MSEE.

"I need your wise counsel, King."

King waved his hand modestly.

"I've got a new guy on board," said Jerzy. "He's one of these special types, like one in ten thousand. A certified genius named Arthur Smith." And Jerzy told King that somehow the HR people had worked a deal with this guy, got him to move over to DataDrive.

"Thing is," said Jerzy, "I don't really want this Smith. I don't need him, know what I mean? I mean, I've got enough creativity with the boys and girls I've got now. But Sammi loves the idea of having this guy." Jerzy did not feel it necessary to tell King that Toni Hunter, that bitch from HR, had come into his office, closed the door, perched on his conference table giving him full frontal thigh, and told him— *told him!*—that he was to take good care of Arthur Smith, who was not under any circumstances to be treated like one of the boys and girls. Sammi himself would not have dared speak to Jerzy that way. So Jerzy knew that someone else was backing Toni. Someone very high. And he thought he knew who that person was. (Of course, he was wrong on all counts. Toni needed no one to back her except Toni Hunter herself.)

"Sammi," said King. "Now there's an empty suit."

"Yeah," said Jerzy, "well he's not going to be there forever. Not from what I hear. But that's another topic. My problem is, what do I give this new guy Smith? Do I give him the Nemo project? Do I shove him into the slush pile and let him sink or swim? Or do I canonize him and just let him do whatever the hell he wants?"

Nemo was supersecret, and except for those working on it, no one outside ExCom plus a handful of top managers was supposed to know about it. But Jerzy knew he could trust King. If you couldn't trust a drinking buddy, who could you trust? he had asked Lisa rhetorically. And she had nodded and smiled. Though Jerzy had told her the bare outlines of Nemo she hadn't understood a word.

"I wouldn't give him Nemo to run," King said thoughtfully, "because to your guys he's an outsider. They'll either give him the freeze or sit back and let him do all the thinking. I'd let him alone for a while. See what he's like. Let him roam through the files. Just be sure he reports directly to you, until you feel him out. You don't want any loose cannons. Or canonized saints."

"There's something else," said Jerzy. "This guy's got a mother."

"Even software guys have got moms," chuckled King.

"Yeah, but this involves complications, sort of. You remember that group I belong to, I was telling you about it some time back?"

"Right," said King. "The Firemen of Liberty, or something."

"Firebrands," said Jerzy. "Anyway, at our general meeting last year celebrating the forty-fifth anniversary of our founding, well, I was in charge of getting the speaker. You know, we wanted the right kind of person. It's getting hard to find the right kind, everyone's getting so soft now that the Commies have given up in Russia."

"Get to the point," said King.

"Well, I wanted Sedge Milbow, you know, the guy on television. He's pretty hot right now."

"The fat guy," said King. "Yeah, he'd be great. But expensive, I'll bet."

"That's just it. He wanted twenty-five grand."

"Jesus!"

"You said it. So I said shit, I can get Felicia Shadroe to come for a whole lot less than that. You know, she writes those columns, beats up on the homos and Democrats."

"And the abortion crowd," added King. "So did she come?"

"Oh yeah, she came. In both senses of the word. I had to be her escort for the evening—she split from her old man years ago. Lisa stayed home, of course. That crowd is too coarse for her. So I ended up plowing Felicia at the airport hotel. Not a bad piece, by the way. Mature, you know what I mean?"

King chuckled.

"The only thing is, she's Arthur Smith's mom."

King stopped chuckling. "Shit, Jerzy—you plugged this guy's mother?"

"At the airport hotel. Her plane was delayed so she got a room for a couple of hours."

King ruminated for a moment, sucking on the last of his Black Russian. Then he said "When she finds out her little boy is working for you, she'll probably take the next plane back here to be sure he gets as good a performance review as you gave her."

"Right," said Jerzy. "By the way, did I tell you about Shirley Wofford?"

King knew the real evening was about to start. "First let's re-up," he said, and signalled to the waitress.

# six

ONI CROSSED THE lobby from the stairs, acknowledging a "good morning" from the girl behind the counter with a curt nod of her head. A week had passed since Arthur Smith had joined the team, and she figured that sufficient time had elapsed for her to make a solicitous inquiry into how things were going. There was something about this man that intrigued her. She hadn't seen him since depositing him into Daphne's care, but she recalled that look he had. Though he had smiled occasionally during their brief time together in her office, she believed that he had some secret sorrow. Something was weighing on his mind, and although Toni had to smile inwardly at the image of herself as a ministering angel, she also had to admit that she was concerned about Arthur Smith.

Toni ran her card through the slot next to the door marked "Laboratory. Admission Restricted." and the door clicked open. Here there was no carpeting, and her heels clicked loudly on the smooth floor. People looked up as she went by their offices, as in this part of the company dilapidated sneakers, or even bare feet, was the rule. Toni had been in the labs only a couple of times, and she had a little trouble finding her way. The downstairs of Building

Fifteen was huge, and corridors crisscrossed each other like the strands of an immense spiderweb. These corridors bore names such as OK Corral, Tombstone Flats and Rattlesnake Gulch. All Toni had to go on was an office number: 115-4-43. But many of the offices lacked numbers and others appeared to have been assigned at random. Finally, as she was despairing of ever finding Arthur she ran into Jerzy Bobochek, who steered her in the right direction and then watched appreciatively and with some bemusement as Toni clicked off down the corridor.

Fenelon was sitting at his desk, on which were piled several files thick with papers. He was doing the crossword puzzle from the San Jose Mercury News, which he found to be not very challenging, but pretty good fun. All three of his computers were on, and each had a display on its screen. Two days before, a very young man with a ponytail and pimples had shown up in his office. He had grunted at Fenelon and had done something to the computers, and presto! the screens had lit up and were promptly filled with lines of text and tiny drawings of various kinds. The young man had then experimented with the little gizmos attached to the computers, running each around on the desktop for a bit. He had then grunted again, only this time it was clearly an attempt at intelligible speech. To Fenelon it sounded something like "mouse dead," though how this adolescent could detect a dead rodent, which must of course be somewhere in the snack room, by manipulating some electronic device in the outer office, Fenelon had no idea.

The young man had disappeared, and Fenelon had assumed he had gone to get a receptacle for carrying away the corpse. Instead he had returned in a minute, carrying another of the little gizmos, which he had attached to the rightmost of the three machines, taking the former one off and slinging it into the wastebasket under the desk.

This time Fenelon could clearly distinguish the words "Dead mouse no value." And a great light had dawned upon him.

He had spent the better part of two days playing with the three computers, and pushing the buttons on what he now knew to be a mouse. He had made some amazing discoveries, not the least of which was that the computer with the largest screen and the finest resolution somehow had access to the most salacious graphical matter Fenelon had ever seen. He realized that this must have been the preoccupation of the former master of the machine who, judging from the images Fenelon was able to conjure up, must have had the most refined tastes in pornography since the 18TH century Japanese master Hashigarumi, some of whose work Fenelon had once seen in an obscure museum in Paris.

The crossword puzzle provided a welcome diversion both from the files, which had materialized mysteriously on Fenelon's chair the second day he showed up for work, and the rather breathtaking display on C3. Fenelon had given each of his computers a number, preceded by a C for computer.

When Toni rapped on the door, Fenelon jumped. He was not expecting any visitors. He stuffed the puzzle into one of the files and opened another at random. Then he remembered C3. But luckily its screen had gone dark. This seemed to happen any time one failed to pay sufficent attention to these things. It must have something to do with saving energy, he had conjectured.

"Come in," called Fenelon, and Toni pushed the door open and came in.

"Hello," she smiled. "Just thought I'd check on how things are going."

Fenelon stood up, and invited Toni to sit at the conference table. He had no idea what to say, but took the initiative anyway.

"How are things in your department?" he asked.

"Things are OK," she said, smiling more brightly than ever. "I've got to confess that your joining us has meant a lot to my career."

"It has?" said Fenelon. "How?"

"You were quite a catch," she said. "I shouldn't tell you this, because it'll just give you a swollen ego, but our group VP, Sammi Boyadjian, got a commendation from Kyle for having brought you on board. Of course, some of the glory rubbed off on me. It looks as if I'm going to be made a director. And really it's all your doing."

Fenelon asked "Who's Kyle?"

Toni stared at him. Then she laughed, not her usual silvery laugh, but a real one. "You are a funny one!" she said. "Everyone in the world knows who Kyle is! At least, if you know *anything* about the industry."

"Yes," said Fenelon.

Toni looked at him. He was really attractive, this strange guy, she thought. Weird, but he's definitely attractive. "Look," she said. "Kyle Winfield is our President and CEO. He's only thirty-six and he's worth a couple of billion. He started this company when he was twenty-five. You *must* know about him."

"Well, I do now," said Fenelon, "and I won't forget him. I promise."

Toni found this utterly charming.

"But getting back to you," said Fenelon, "I'm very happy that things are going well for you."

"Yes," Toni said. "And they don't always, you know. People here hate the HR function, and it's hard working when you're always a, well, sort of like...."

"An object of obloquy?" Fenelon prompted helpfully.

Toni felt confused. "Well, maybe," she said. "I can't blame people for hating us, though. We're constantly sending these mixed messages. Like we have these celebrations when a group of employees gets to their fifth anniversary with the company. They get a lunch with Kyle, funny hats, a speech, a day off and a gold seal to put on their badges or send to their mothers or whatever. And whenever we have a big company event, training workshop, anything like that, we always have these great T-shirts made up for the occasion."

"That's very nice," said Fenelon. "It's like belonging to a family."

"Yes," said Toni, "but at the same time we're also sending a different message. We're telling everyone that they've gotta be like entrepreneurs. They're responsible for their own careers. We give 'em a salary and the chance for training, but we specifically tell them they are *not* part of a family. See, a family helps you out when things get rough."

"Get rough?" said Fenelon in a questioning tone.

"Yes," said Toni. This conversation was doing her a lot of good. She could feel emotions coming out that had been suppressed for a long time. "I mean, like downsizing, or rightsizing, or layoffs, or a massacre of the innocents if that's what you want to call it. And they are innocents, the ones that end up out on the street. Innocent because all they do is their jobs."

"But isn't that what they're paid for?" asked Fenelon.

"Yes, Arthur, they are. But I'm sure you know better than anyone how fast things are changing in the industry. People become stale. Their knowledge becomes outdated, and if they don't keep up, well, then out they go."

"So let them keep up," said Fenelon.

"It's not so simple," Toni said. "We've got this concept called core competencies. That's all the stuff that this company does better than anyone in the whole world. We'll never outsource our core competencies, because that's what defines us. But the skills needed to service these competencies, that's what people need to keep current. Now, you might think that all we'd have to do is publish a list of these core competencies and what people would have to do to keep up to date."

"That's just what I was thinking," said Fenelon, who in fact was still grappling with the word "outsource," and finding it completely lacking in charm.

"Yes," Toni said, "that would make sense. Except we've tried to make a list of our core competencies lots of times, and we've never succeeded. The lists we come up with look so stupid we've never dared publicize them. In fact if we ever did, they might even be used against us some day in a suit for wrongful termination. So the employees are under pressure to measure up to a standard that is not only vague, it doesn't really exist at all."

"So where does that leave the employees?"

"Well, those that play the political game are OK," Toni replied. "And there are a few top people, like the top sales people, or the top techies. You, for example, Arthur. You have nothing to fear." So saying she pushed her chair back and stood up. She had not intended to say all these things to Arthur Smith, but he was such a damned good listener! Toni felt a need to cover her tracks. She had made herself vulnerable to this man, and felt exposed. She stepped over to Fenelon's desk and stood in front of C3. "I guess you've had some time to start some thought processes going," she said, smiling over at him. "Mind if I take a peek?"

And before Fenelon could move a muscle Toni had pressed the spacebar on the keyboard of C3.

C3 was, of course, a 32-bit machine, with 20 megs of RAM, a 1.2 gigabyte hard disk, and a screen with 1280 by 1084 resolution and 1.2 million colors available. All of these features leaped into action as soon as Toni's finger had depressed the spacebar by a millimeter or so. The screen sprang into life.

Toni was still looking at Fenelon, who was staring at the screen. A brief glimpse of the screen, say for the space of a nanosecond, might have given the viewer the impression that he—or she—was looking at a display of quivering tropical fruit, or perhaps a dish of exotic live mollusks. But as Toni turned to glance at the image her gaze seemed to lock onto the screen for much longer than a nanosecond.

Fenelon remembered his Boy Scout survival training. "Remain calm," was rule number one. So he kept a bland expression, though inside he was churning. He felt he had to make some kind of non-committal remark. "Of course, that's not the only research I'm conducting," he heard himself say.

Toni couldn't seem to tear her eyes away from the screen. She said "Arthur, you are a man full of surprises. We ought to discuss this."

Fenelon felt that any attempt at explanation would be futile. "I suppose you'd like me to go with you to your office," he said in a low voice.

Toni kept staring at the screen. "Are you mad?" she said, and her voice too was low, and perhaps a bit unsteady. "Not in my office. In the next room."

"You mean the room with the vending machines?" Fenelon said.

"I mean," said Toni, finally looking away from the screen and directly into Fenelon's eyes, "I mean, the room with the futon."

IN THE MEANTIME, Carmelita had returned from her break and was gabbing with Trudi behind the receptionist's counter. In the past week Carmelita had broken up with Kurt, who had confessed to a brief affair with a burgerflipper he had met at a fast food joint late one night. Carmelita had been so angry she had read the riot act to Kurt in Spanish. There were times when only Spanish seemed to fill the bill. Kurt had been in anguish for two days, because he really loved Carmelita but had let himself be momentarily led astray. He sent Carmelita two dozen roses, and the next day a very pretty charm from Gump's. Carmelita knew Kurt must have gotten out of bed very early in his day to make it up to the city to Gump's, and then back in time for work at the Silicon Corral. She appreciated this gesture more than she could say, and so after she was sure that Kurt had sufficiently abased himself and that she had control of things again, she allowed herself to relent. Kurt was so happy that he considered proposing marriage to Carmelita. She was very beautiful and very fiery, which was what Kurt liked. Kurt thought that if he still felt the same way in a few weeks he'd pop the question.

So Carmelita was in a very good mood as she sat and chatted with Trudi, who was trying to read a textbook on organic chemistry. Finally Trudi had to give it up. She closed the book with a sigh.

"By the way," she said. "Toni's in the lab. Just so you know." This was so that Carmelita wouldn't be surprised by Toni's sudden emergence in the lobby from an unexpected direction.

"The lab?" said Carmelita. "What's she doing in the lab?"

"Research, maybe," said Trudi. "She's been in there at least half an hour."

"Research my Aunt Corazon," said Carmelita. "I bet I know. She's visiting you-know-who." She was silent for a moment and then said "I bet she's got her claws into that guy already."

Trudi shrugged. She was getting ready to go.

"Look," said Carmelita. "You stay here another minute or two. I'm going to see what's up."

"Are you nuts?" said Trudi, her eyes widening. "We can't go in there!"

"But I will," said Carmelita. "If anyone stops me I'll say I'm trying to find Jerzy. That'll shut 'em up."

"Yeah," Trudi snorted. "And if you run into Jerzy?"

"He won't bother me," said Carmelita with a grin. "Except he'll try to get me into his office." She reached for the phone and dialed a number. "Hello, Helen? Carmelita. Yeah, another guy forgot his badge. Hank Dalton. Yeah, I know. Buzz him in, will ya?"

She stood up and ran over to the lab door, which buzzed just as she reached it. Turning the handle she winked at Trudi and disappeared into the lab.

Carmelita was gone maybe four minutes. Then she reappeared.

"Did you see Toni?" asked Trudi.

"Well," said Carmelita, "I saw parts of Toni. And parts of Arthur Smith. It was all sort of jumbled up."

Trudi was awestruck. "That's bullshit!" she blurted out.

"Oh no it's not, *mi querida!*" said Carmelita with a giggle. "They've put a sort of mail slot into the office door. I could see right into a kind of inner room. They were in there, on some kind of mattress."

"Mattress?" goggled Trudi. "In the lab?"

"In an inner room. They were making it in front of two vending machines."

"Vending machines?"

"That's what I said."

The two women were silent for a few minutes, each with her own thoughts. Trudi was excited by the thought that illicit sex was going on not fifty feet from where she sat, at eleven in the morning. Carmelita was wishing she had brought her pocket camera with her and was wondering whether or not to entrust Kurt with this story. She knew he had a tendency to spread things around. Her mother had told her more than once "If you want to keep a secret, don't tell anyone," and Carmelita had always followed this rule. Except for the things she confided to Trudi, of course, who could certainly keep a secret.

Suddenly Trudi stood up. "I've got to get going," she said. "I've got an organic chemistry quiz at five, and I've got two chapters to do."

"There's plenty of organic chemistry going on in the lab," Carmelita said, laughing. "Take it easy. I'll see you at three and let you know what she looks like when she comes out. If she comes out, that is."

# seven

ARTHUR SMITH HAD spent a wonderful four days at his mother's condo in Aspen. The ride out had taken longer than he had planned—twenty days. Hitherto the longest trip Arthur had ever taken on his bicycle had been from his apartment to the video store on El Camino, a distance of about three miles. And there hadn't been any mountains in the way. Arthur had been a bit out of shape when he started the trip. But he had lost weight en route and looked pretty good, if tired, when he wheeled through the imposing stone gates of Styx Manor. His mother had vowed to "fatten him up," as he no longer looked like her baby boy. Felicia Shadroe, who had reverted to her maiden name when she had divorced Arthur's dad, looked much younger than her forty-nine years, but it didn't help to have a lean, windburned thirty-year-old son hanging about the place. Arthur podgy looked as if he might be twenty at the most. Arthur fit made her look, well, older than she wanted to look.

Arthur had recounted his distress at the change in snack vendors, and how he had confronted the VP of Siegfried Software in the parking lot. Felicia had cooed and gasped at appropriate moments, while feeding Arthur doughnut holes from Swanleigh's bakery. When Arthur told her about Judd's wooing of him her eyes glistened with proud tears. But when Arthur told her he had agreed to work for DataDrive she became subdued. This was not an habitual state for Felicia, and Arthur naturally inquired of his mother what could be wrong.

"It's nothing, darling," she said. "It's just that I know something about the people in that company. I am not sure they can be trusted. How much did you say they are paying you?"

Arthur, of course, could not expound on this subject, as he had never discussed the matter with Judd. Whereupon Felicia told Arthur he must fly immediately to San Jose and settle the matter with the powers that be at DataDrive. "And if you have any trouble with, well, with anyone high up in the software division, you just let me know."

Felicia arranged an air ticket for her son and gave him a hundred dollars to pay for a cab from San Jose airport to his apartment. Then she had to dash off to an appointment at a radio station. It was then that Arthur thought of his bicycle. He did not want to entrust it to the hold of an airplane. He and it had been through too much together. He called the airport, canceled his flight, and thoughtfully put the ticket on his mother's favorite wing chair where she would be sure to find it. He put his spare clothes into his saddlebags, stuffed the hundred dollars into the pocket of his shorts, and pedalled off toward California.

# eight

I T  H A D  B E E N three weeks since Fenelon had come to work at DataDrive as Arthur Smith. Toni had visited him six more times to go over some documents and conduct other business. She had not seemed interested in seeing Fenelon off the premises, and it was likely, he thought, that she had outside commitments that discouraged extracurricular rendezvous. Fenelon surmised that the fact that these visits occurred during working hours also provided a stimulus to Toni's imagination which heightened her enjoyment of sex. The thought of doing it while others unwittingly toiled nearby was the turn-on. Fenelon was unaware that there were at least two witting observers of Toni's goings and comings. These were Trudi and Carmelita. Carmelita had brought her little camera with her to work every day, just in case, and this foresight paid off the Tuesday morning following Toni's first visit.

Things had not been going too badly for Fenelon on the work front either, inasmuch as there seemed to be no work to do. Fenelon had learned how to work the electronic mail on C2 and had tried sending off a few tentative messages. C3 had been cleared of its lubricious displays by the simple method of pulling the plug and casting the whole machine into darkness. C1's screen was filled with fantastical symbols and letters which appeared to be arranged into word-like groups, but which were totally devoid of meaning so far as Fenelon could see. He kept them there nonetheless, as he felt that it lent his office a slight aura of research which might come in handy some day.

He had discovered that during the day the labs were but sparsely populated, and he had wondered where all the employees could be. But one evening, after a movie, he had stopped off at the lab to pick up a few bags of Kachina corn chips, to which he was becoming rather addicted. To his surprise, the parking lot was filled with cars, motorcycles, and bicycles. He entered the lab and found a beehive of activity. Many people he did not recognize greeted him with a nod, while others scuttled by him sideways in the corridor like so many crabs. Fenelon went to his office to get the chips and to think things over. He began to realize that, at least at DataDrive, the software people were night people. "Like cicadas, they must be more creative at night," he mused. He opened a bag of Kachina chips and had hardly begun to munch when there came a knock on the door. Fenelon checked his watch. It couldn't be Toni, because it was after nine p.m. He got up and opened the door.

Outside there stood a strange-looking man of perhaps thirty, who was obviously crippled. His short body was bent to one side, and his thin face was likewise canted, so that he peered sideways up at Fenelon. He was thin, almost emaciated, and with his dark skin he looked like a caricature of a beggar in some crowded street in India, except that he wore a dark blue cashmere sweater with the DataDrive badge clipped to the V lapel.

"You're Arthur Smith," said the man, and thrust out his hand. "I am Ranjan Chatterjee. May I come in?" His hand was large, and he squeezed Fenelon's with surprising strength. Fenelon closed the door after him and indicated the conference table.

"You're the first visitor I've had," he said. "Well, almost the first."

"That's because you're never at work," said Chatterjee, smiling.

"I've been coming during the day, when there's almost no one here."

Chatterjee swung his head and thin shoulders around and surveyed the room. "I see you go for Kachinas," he observed.

Fenelon held out the bag of corn chips he had just been starting on. "Want some?" he inquired.

"Don't mind if I do," said Chatterjee. "My favorite snack."

Fenelon had been dreading the first visit from one of his supposed colleagues, but now that it was actually happening it seemed to have all the menace and drama of a sedate Victorian tea party. Chatterjee appeared to be quite relaxed as he munched on the chips, the cellophane bag crackling a bit as he thrust into it with his long fingers.

"Well," said the Indian, "I was wondering what you think of Nemo."

Fenelon said "I haven't met him yet."

Chatterjee seemed to find this remark extremely funny. He chuckled in delight. "That is good! Really, very very good! Ah-h! You have a sense of humor. We need some of that around here."

Fenelon cast caution to the winds. "I meant what I said. I assume that this Nemo is someone I ought to know, but I don't. You're the first person I've met in the whole lab in three weeks."

Perplexity sprang into Chatterjee's small, dark features. "Didn't you get the files I left on your chair? You've had them for several days now. I was hoping we could have a discussion about the project."

"Nemo is a project?" said Fenelon, who was beginning to espy a glimmer of light. "So you were the person who left all this stuff." And he gestured toward the shelf over the desk, where reposed the stack of files.

"Yes, yes!" Chatterjee said eagerly. "Did you get through them?"

"Not exactly," said Fenelon. "I glanced at them, but..." and here he hesitated. He could make up a story of some kind to get rid of this man, or he could lie and say he hadn't had time to digest the contents of the files. Or he could even tell the truth.

Chatterjee interrupted his thought. "You see, Arthur, I'm in charge of Nemo. I know someone, maybe Jerzy, must have briefed you on it."

"No one has briefed me on anything," said Fenelon. "Really, I know nothing about it."

Chatterjee said "Do you mind if I have some more Kachina chips?"

"Take all you want," said Fenelon. "There's a vending machine in that room. You can get stuff without paying."

"That's very very nice," said Chatterjee, and he scurried into the adjoining room and soon returned with three cellophane bags. "You have a futon in there, I see. For meditation, I suppose."

"Tell me about Nemo," said Fenelon, accepting a handful of Kachina chips that Chatterjee shook into his hand from the bag.

"Nemo," said Chatterjee dreamily. "It is going to be the greatest contribution to information flow since... since...," and he stopped, overcome. "It is full-blown nomadic information processing, with unbelievable power. Graphics, voice, data, immense memory storage. Not a wire to be seen. A unit the size of a credit card, configured for the individual, with all one's personal data, bank accounts, car license, registration, and so on. It will be dockable in cheap units which will be available everywhere—on buses, in cars, on airplanes, in hotels and restaurants—in every telephone, in fact. It will be freely licensed, of course. A unique operating system yet fully compatible with virtually every UNIX and MS-DOS application."

He stopped again and looked at Fenelon. "And I am responsible for all the software side. I have a team of six hundred engineers, and I have a deadline. A deadline of October 30, Arthur. That is when the beta version is due. And so far things are not going well. There are some barriers that seem insurmountable. That is why I need your help. I do not care about myself. I shall always make a living, and in any case my family has money in India. I can always return there. But for the others it will be bad. They will be out. Out!" and at this point Chatterjee waved both his hands in the air.

Fenelon made a decision. "I would like to help," he said, slowly. "I really would. But you see, I can't, because I know nothing, nothing at all about computers, or software, or anything like that."

Chatterjee looked at him keenly. "I see," he said. "You are not Arthur Smith."

"No," said Fenelon. "Arthur Smith is a software genius. I am a teacher of French language and literature, and not a very good one, at that."

"And where is Arthur Smith?" said Chatterjee. "Have you done away with him?"

"Good God, no! I have no idea where he is. He was supposed to show up the day I did, but he seems to have vanished into thin air."

"And how did you happen to show up in the first place?" asked Chatterjee.

"I had to take a leak," said Fenelon.

"Yes, I see," said Chatterjee. "Excuse me, but is the drink machine also free? Or must one pay?"

"No, it's free. Everything is free."

Chatterjee got up and again went to the rear room, returning with two plastic bottles of juice. He removed the top of one of the bottles and drank from it. "This is very good stuff," he said. "Well, it appears you will not be able to help me much with Nemo."

"I said I'm sorry," said Fenelon.

"By the way, what is your name?" asked the Indian.

"My name is Fenelon. My friends used to call me Fen, or sometimes Fenny."

"Why do you say 'used to' in that way? What do they call you now?"

"I have no friends out here," said Fenelon wearily.

Chatterjee drummed his long fingers on the conference table for a minute. Then he said "It is ten o'clock. I am very hungry. Do you like Indian food?"

"I've never had any," said Fenelon.

"Then we had better remedy that as soon as possible. Do you have a car? If so, I will direct you to the best Indian restaurant on the Peninsula. It is owned by a cousin. He will be very glad to see us. Come on. They close at eleven, and I am really very hungry."

IT WAS ELEVEN-THIRTY. Fenelon was stuffed. He lolled in his chair at the Silk Saree and belched contentedly. Across from him Ranjan Chatterjee thoughtfully picked his teeth. Fenelon's introduction to Indian food was one of those processes of discovery that are never to be forgotten, like one's first seduction, except that the afterglow of an Indian dinner is of longer duration and usually proves less expensive. At first Fenelon had worried about what might be in each dish, and had asked details of Chatterjee until the latter's patience had been sorely tried. He had suggested that Fenelon use his mouth solely for eating. So Fenelon had shelved his Indiana inhibitions and fears and had tucked in with a will. He had never tasted anything so delicious. Until that evening the spiciest food he had consumed had been a half-smoke purchased from a street vendor in front of the Palo Alto post office. The range, the depth of flavor of Indian cuisine overpowered him with delight.

"That was fabulous," he said.

"It was fairly good, for restaurant cooking," said Chatterjee. "Not to be compared with the home variety, of course."

Fenelon laughed. "You mean there's better than this?"

"Some day I will take you to my home. My sister will cook dinner for us. Then you will see."

"I would like that very much. But first I need a month to recuperate from tonight."

Chatterjee smiled. "You will see. Tomorrow morning already you will be hungry. Will you have tea now?"

"Good idea," said Fenelon.

THE TEA HAD arrived. Fenelon could see that he and Chatterjee were the only persons left in the restaurant, other than a bored-looking waiter who lolled against a back wall. From the kitchen came occasional muffled voices.

Chatterjee seemed in no hurry to end the evening. "Tell me about yourself," he said. "You are, or were, a teacher in Indiana. Why did you leave?"

"Some things went wrong," said Fenelon.

"Yes," said Chatterjee.

"They say, you know, that bad news comes in threes. And that's what happened in my case. First, I didn't get tenure. If my doctorate had been from some place like Yale or Stanford, things might have worked out differently. But it was from one of the big midwestern universities. As they say, no man is a prophet in his own land. And no new Ph.D. is worth a damn in the midwest if his degree is also from the midwest."

"Aha," said Chatterjee.

Fenelon poured himself some more tea. "I put out the effort all right. I taught everything from survey courses to the poetry of Villon and Marot, to the nineteenth century novels. Are you up on the nineteenth century?"

"Not at all," said Chatterjee. "Universities in India are quite deficient when it comes to nineteenth century French literature."

"I only published three articles in five years," said Fenelon moodily. "That can do you in, you know. Also, I got involved in one of those academic arguments during a plenary session of the MLA. That's the Modern Language Association. I took the wrong side in a fight over Haitian patois and other varieties of French. The issue was whether literature written in those dialects should be taught as part of the mainstream, or whether they ought to be put into the Black Studies program."

"Very interesting," said Chatterjee. "And which side did you take in this debate?"

"The losing side. It doesn't matter what I thought, really. When you get into these kinds of issues they quickly become political, and the knives come out. I don't think our dean appreciated the publicity. Though it hardly made the *New York Times*."

"I think I will have some kulfi," said Chatterjee. "It is a sort of Indian ice cream. I suggest you try it." And he gestured to the waiter, who hurried over.

"You said there were three bad things," he said, after the dessert was ordered. "What were the other two, if I may ask?"

"My wife left me," said Fenelon. "We'd always gotten along pretty well, and I'm still grappling with what happened. It was one morning, the kids were off to school and I was sipping coffee, going over my notes for my ten o'clock. She just rapped on her cup with a spoon, the way you do to get an audience to quiet down. Then she told me she was leaving. And she went on and on about the house, and the kids, and a lot of other things."

"Why did she do such a thing?" asked Chatterjee.

"I've thought and thought about it. She never really came out with a reason, but I guess a lot of stuff had built up over the years. She was tearful and angry. I was pretty taken up with my own career problems, and we just had grown apart. Maybe I was trying to do too much at the college. She was working for this firm of lawyers as a secretary, and one of the things she told me was she was going to become a lawyer. That was the first I heard of it." Fenelon finished his tea as the waiter arrived with the desserts.

"And the third thing that happened?" said Chatterjee.

# nine

HAD ALWAYS KIDDED Antje, my soon-to-be ex-wife, about her need to visit every toilet facility on the Indiana Turnpike when we made our bimonthly pilgrimages to visit her mother in Monrovia. I used to tell our friends that she had the smallest bladder in the Midwest. You might have though that Antje would have been offended at these remarks, but she was pretty tolerant of me and never said anything about it. Indeed, after a while, Antje herself picked up this line and used to trot it out whenever we were with new acquaintances and she had to drop everything to dash off to the nearest facility, or bush. In fact, when we would go to the movies she'd have to dash from the car while it was still in our driveway and run for the house to pee "just in case" as she said; then she'd have to go again as soon as we reached the theatre, even if traffic was light and we'd made it in fifteen minutes. I, on the other hand, could hold it forever. Once I had to drive to Columbus for a meeting and I thought I was going to be late. So even though I had had four cups of coffee before getting behind the wheel (it was very early in the morning, and I wanted to be sure to stay awake), I drove straight through—a trip of five hours—and wasn't aware I had to go at all until I had reached my destination.

Then I had to read that damned article about this gland, which, like the oil dipstick on my Chevy, is located in an almost inaccessible area somewhere back of beyond; and though I was still a few years from the dangerous age (I'm only thirty-nine), I started to think about it. To obsess, as Antje would say, in that way she has of turning nouns into verbs, and jargonistic verbs at that. I once lightly raised the issue of the prostate with Antje. I mean, of course, prostate in a general sense, not my own. To my intense annoyance she instantly leaped to the conclusion that I had some sort of concern about my own, whereas I didn't at all. Antje said "If you're worried, I suggest you see a doctor and get an examination." Just like that! Then she went right on making toast, or doing whatever in the kitchen. I laughed, of course, and told her I wasn't at all concerned. I just wanted to discuss an article I'd read, that was all. Examination! Bending over and letting some medico slide a greased finger up my butt! Not likely!

Of course, what Antje did was somehow plant this fear in me that maybe I was wrong not to be concerned about my prostate. You know how something can get into your head and then it's damned hard to get it out. Like a few years ago when I had trouble getting an erection. Well, I was terrified that I was impotent. That time I must admit Antje was pretty helpful. She's always reading this five-foot shelf of helpful literature on everything that could go wrong with the psyche. One reason our family budget never seemed to work was that she felt impelled to buy and read all the works of every psychologist and would-be psychologist that dealt with self-improvement, relationships, birth, death, and every emotion in between. On the salary of an associate professor of French language and literature that's a very heavy load to bear, even if we got a substantial discount at the college bookstore.

Anyway, Antje talked me into relaxing about the whole thing, the erection came back and *ipso facto* the problem went away. It was all in the mind, as my mother used to say. Of course, she was talking in a general sense, not about erections. Though I was close to

my mother I hadn't ever alluded to the erection problem while I
was around her.

Anyway, to get back to our sheep, as Molière says, I began to read
everything I could find about the prostate, and about drug therapy,
and cancer, and operations and survival rates. One thing I discovered reassured me somewhat: prostate cancer hits black men a lot
harder than anyone else. Not that I wished ill to black men, but
that's the way it was. It tipped the statistical balance a bit more in
my favor. And as I say, I was still fairly far from the dangerous age
for PC.

On the other hand there are exceptions to every medical rule. I
read about that in some magazine I was leafing through at my dentist's office. When you're waiting to see the dentist your sensibilities
are increased all around, even if you're only there for a routine
cleaning and inspection. My dentist was very popular and had
three hygienists. The first couple of times I went I got one of the
ugly ones. She had reddish hair, which I would have loved had it
been fuller and not so stringy. And she had a long horsey face and
narrow eyes, of the kind the novelists call "piercing." She could
make you feel that you had to bring a written note from your wife
attesting to your flossing regularly. The next time I went to the dentist's, the redheaded hygienist was ill, and I found myself being
greeted at the door of the little room by a vision in white. Her name
was Paula, and she was (as I soon found out) twenty-six. She had
the most beautiful face, like a madonna's, with a natural glow that
had to come from lots of outdoor exercise. Her hair was dark
blonde, but—I can't explain it—but somehow it was more toward
gray than brown. And yet it wasn't gray. I couldn't figure it out. Her
eyes were definitely green. I looked into them a lot while she was
bending over me, working on my teeth. Paula was fairly tall, maybe
five seven or a bit more, and her figure was slim. The tantalizing
thing was, she wore these white trousers and usually a yellow or
green sweater and then some kind of smock over them. So it wasn't
really possible to tell what she would have looked like without

clothes; you had to imagine. And whenever I was looking elsewhere other than into those green eyes I did imagine.

Now I don't want you to think that I'm some kind of sex maniac. For one thing, we don't have any of those in Indiana, at least not outside Indianapolis. But I have to say that getting my teeth cleaned was becoming a highly erotic experience. Maybe that is the reason I increased the number of visits to the dentist from two per year to four.

Anyway, I was waiting to see Paula and was leafing through this magazine which was about three or four months out of date, and what should I see but an article about unusual medical cases. I suppose the dentist put stuff like that in the waiting room to take your mind off what lay ahead. I was reading in a desultory way about all these strange exceptions to the norm. Girls that get breast cancer at age seventeen. A colony of reclusive Christian farmers in Kentucky, none of whom were related, all of whom had some strange blood disease (not sickle cell, though). Hyperactive children who were raised near high-tension power lines. Men in their thirties and forties who get prostate cancer. That woke me up, I can tell you! I tried to concentrate on the forthcoming encounter with Paula, when I would be under her ministering hands. But it didn't work. All I could think of was that if one put one's faith in statistics I still had a few years before the tiger would be at the gate. I kept thinking that maybe Antje was right, that I should see a doctor, but it was inconvenient to do so. Anyway the doctor we had, I mean our GP, who was the only doctor we had (GPs still exist, though an endangered species, in Indiana), was a woman.

Now I'm as liberated as any man, or at least as any man born and raised in western Indiana. Our doctor is very professional, and I'm certainly not embarrassed to appear before her with my pants down, so to speak. She's about my age, married to a businessman, and has two kids who are about seven and five years old. She's pretty attractive, too. Long dark hair, dark blue eyes, very clear complexion, and long caring fingers, the way a doctor's ought to be. In fact, come to think of it I *have* appeared before her with my pants down, because the college required a physical exam once a year of all faculty and staff, and that included probing for a hernia. The first time Dr. Bonham (her first name is Clara, but I never dared call her that; the one thing about dental hygienists is that you can call them by their first names from the start) was probing me to see if anything had slipped its bounds, I was quite relaxed. As I recall we were talking about the Colts' prospects for the coming season. They weren't very good, it seemed. Dr. Bonham followed sports more than I did, so I had to take her word for it. Anyway I was busy coughing when she told me to cough, and hoping that my renascent erective powers wouldn't manifest themselves at that precise moment. And they didn't.

Well, I didn't have a hernia, not that year, nor any year for the five years thereafter. Dr. Bonham, on my last visit, which was just about a year ago and shortly after I had started to become really knowledgeable about the prostate, suggested that I have an exam then and there. I must have mentioned something to her about my medical reading, and probably she, like Antje, had concluded that I had some kind of worry, or phobia. I demurred to her suggestion, pleading a lack of time. I just couldn't see how I could bend over and present my ass to Dr. Bonham, though I suppose had it been a question of a boil I could have done it. After all, boils are within a GP's purview, as it were. But my prostate was different. I knew from my reading that it was about walnut size, which seemed to me obscene, I don't know why. What was anything that large doing tucked away up there? I did not want to have one of her caring fingers probing it, not only because it smacked of perversity (though come to think of it you could say as much, or more, about a male doctor's finger), but because her caring fingers had very long, red fingernails. I just didn't see how it could be accomplished with any degree either of dignity or of comfort.

So, as I say, I demurred as diplomatically as I could, though I am not sure she didn't see through my murmured excuse and my glancing at my watch. As she said goodbye, I thought I caught a glimmer of something like amusement in those blue eyes. But I might have imagined it.

When Antje and I separated, in the end it was I who moved out. I went to spend the final months of the academic year with my friend Emile Fortier, who does the sixteenth and seventeenth centuries as well as a Comp. Lit. seminar. Emile is French and doesn't have a wife. The humanities part of the college library is rather deep underground, perhaps reflecting its status as compared with that of the engineering department, for example, and sometimes I feel that Emile never spent enough time aboveground to have developed any kind of normal relations with anyone inhabiting the upper world. He only seems to emerge late at night, like a mole. Emile is much older than I am. I think he's in his mid-fifties, and I'm sure he's never had any kind of extensive normal, or for that matter abnormal, sexual relationship. He seems wedded to Montaigne, so to speak.

Emile and I got along very well during those months. He would arrive about midnight, and I could hear him on the sidewalk (my room was the den, at the front of the house), as he fumbled for his keys, dropping files on the front step and muttering muffled Gallic curses as he bent to retrieve them, dropping more papers in the process. On more than one occasion I was in bed with one or another of a small coterie of young female students, mostly undergrads (though we did have a Master's program, in which I also taught), who admired my classroom style, who had learned of the separation, and who desired a closer acquaintance with me. Whichever one I would happen to be with that evening would usually have to stifle giggles as the sounds of Emile's return reached us. I'm not certain what Emile's reaction would have been had he heard any untoward noises and chosen to investigate. I didn't think he was a prude, but I didn't want it to get about the campus that I was working off my anger at Antje this way. What I didn't know was that it was already all over the campus. Looking back I can see how naive I was, thinking that you can keep anything secret in a college town. In fact, there appears in retrospect to have been some kind of competition among some elements of the female student population to see who could most frequent my boudoir in the remainder of the year. I suppose I'm reasonably attractive for my age, and dealing with these young admirers was, I guess, the price I had to pay for working out regularly at the gym and jogging every morning, and therefore being in fairly good physical shape. Psychologically I felt terrible, but I kept exercising. I felt I had to or I wouldn't be able to get out of bed each morning. Being a lame duck teacher didn't of itself provide any motivation.

THE THIRD BAD thing that happened to me, and the one that convinced me to leave Terre Haute, was that I ran out of money. Antje had worked as a receptionist in a downtown law firm. She started at around nine o'clock, but they liked her so well that if she had an emergency of some kind (such as the morning she told me our marriage was over), she had only to call and the firm would actually put one of the young associates on phone duty until she could make it in to the office. Antje didn't make a lot of money at her job, but somehow she seemed to have been able to put enough aside to be confident of survival without me. In fact, I didn't even know how much money she made. Mine was the paycheck that covered all the family expenses, including all those self-awareness and self-help books she had amassed. I was therefore surprised when, during that morning conference at which I had started out my contribution to the discussion by choking on the toast, I introduced the subject of the doubtfulness of her economic survival, and she hadn't blenched at all.

"I have enough," was all that she said, and I admit that I was intrigued by her enigmatic phrase. How one can introduce enigma into a phrase of only three words I cannot explain. I only report what I felt.

It soon transpired, however, that "I have enough" spoken by Antje included an unspoken, but heartfelt "and so do you, Fenelon." I received a letter, hand-delivered to Emile's front step, and signed for by me, from a man whose name I vaguely recalled as being that of one of the quondam phone sitters for Antje at the law firm. This letter was professional, its tone brisk and cool, but not unfriendly. Its contents were unpleasant, however, chiefly having to do with the forthcoming divorce and consequent disposition of my assets. I spoke with a friend who taught law at UI. "My advice is to take the *res* and run," he said in a jocular manner. I didn't understand precisely what a res was, and in any case he didn't seem to be very interested in my case. As it turned out, he taught a subject called "Trusts." My problems didn't seem to involve that area of the law, except that I considered that Antje had betrayed my trust.

I didn't know any lawyers other than a few I'd met at the Christmas parties to which Antje dragged me at her firm. I wasn't sure how professional ethics worked among lawyers, though I suspected the worst. Could I hire a lawyer who worked in the same firm as Antje? If I did, could I rely on him not to share his thoughts with the lawyer representing her? Antje, through all those books she had read, had developed what one might in these modern times call a "thing" about "sharing." "Sharing" was good. It led to harmony, she said, though from what little I knew of the subject, it as often led to bitterness, accusations and remorse. Perhaps Antje's philosophy had infected the firm. Perhaps all these attorneys spent a brief moment every morning holding hands in a circle around the table in the large conference room (the same room where they held the Christmas revels), and each one got a minute or two to share what was on his mind.

But no, that wouldn't do, as it was a largish firm, some eighty lawyers, I believe. Even the large conference room could not have held them all at once, especially standing around in a circle. And it would have consumed too many billable hours for the senior partners to stomach. Though I was aware that a lawyer's day can easily contain more billable hours than a sidereal day I still came to the conclusion that sharing was out.

As it happened I didn't have to worry about getting my own lawyer. Antje made the very sensible suggestion that if I were to find her lawyer's financial and familial proposals reasonable, I could just say so and I would be spared the expense of paying for legal services. Raymond, her counsel, was quite experienced in divorce settlements and would be evenhanded and fair.

I suppose I was just plain tired of it all. I said yes. I left everything to Raymond. That turned out to be a mistake. As a result I found myself one day with about three hundred fifty dollars in my bank account, another fifteen or so in my pocket, my aging Chevrolet, and some twenty cartons of books and papers as my total worldly assets. I talked it over with Emile that night, one I remember well, because I had turned away not one, but two pretty French majors from Emile's door by the time he returned from the nether world of the library stacks.

I had stopped shaving a few weeks before and had a sort of scraggy beard of the sort the French call a *collier*. I had also not been eating too well and had lost weight, though continuing to run and work out, which is supposed to give you an appetite. My leather jacket, which I had originally affected because I thought that in it I resembled Jean Genet, whom I was reading at the time, was out at both elbows. I also wore a thin yellow woolen scarf, the ends of which were sometimes whipped about by the wind as I crossed the campus. The unintended, but apparently powerful effect of all this was actually to make me look more like the fifteenth century rogue poet François Villon than Genet, who in any case was homosexual, as I was not.

For several days I had been pursued by the two pretty girls mentioned, both of whom were in my Villon/Marot class. One I was already familiar with, having known her the previous semester in *Oeuvres Principales du XIXème Siècle*. Her rival was a transfer from a junior college, and so she was new to the campus and to me. These girls—I can say "girls" now that Antje's not listening, and besides neither was over twenty—almost ran into one another as they came and left Emile's house. So when Emile finally showed up I was nervous and under some strain. We had a talk.

"*Mon cher* Fenelon," said Emile. "This town has nothing for you. Nothing." (He had been in this country for twenty-five years, but still pronounced it "nuzzing.") "You must leave. What have you heard?"

He meant what had I heard from the three hundred or so inquiries *cum* resumés I had sprayed about the academic landscape.

"Nothing," I said, pronouncing it correctly.

"Then you must consider the private schools."

Emile meant by this the private secondary schools, and there was no denying that there were jobs to be had for Ph.Ds in such places, even Ph.Ds from the midwest.

"I can't do it, Emile," I said. "I can't isolate myself in some high-priced academy for spoiled rich kids." My favorite uncle had worked on the production line in Dearborn, Michigan, for almost a quarter century, and politically I've always considered myself a New Dealer, though I know that's out of fashion. In fact, the New Deal never was in fashion in Indiana. "Besides which...."

Emile waited courteously, but I said nothing. I had been about to say "Besides which, the female students in a private high school would be a lot more dangerous than at a college." I meant the age question, of course.

"*Mon ami*, you have no choice," said Emile gravely. "Times are hard. They will get better someday, but now...." He let the silence say the rest.

Emile came originally from Poitou, which is the cradle of French hospitality according to him. I had studied in France for a year and had been back twice on vacation, but had never been to Poitou. I had never thought of the French as being hospitable to

any marked degree, but Emile's conduct toward me during this trying time in my life showed that at least one Frenchman could be
generous to a fault. It was only after some persuading that he had
agreed to accept a hundred dollars a month toward household
expenses. But now I was running so low on cash that I couldn't see
how to meet next month's contribution. It was clear that I had to
act.

The next morning I rose early and did a wash of all the dirty
clothes that had piled up in the closet. I threw everything in together—reds, blues, whites, blacks. Up to that point I had been
scrupulous about following Antje's prescripts in the matter of sep-
arating colors. But the way I felt on this, my final morning at
Emile's and in Terre Haute, I was quite ready for everything to
come out of the wash a uniformly muddy ochre. Strangely enough,
though, all the colors seemed to have retained their distinctive hues
when I finally fished the clothes out of the machine and put them
in the dryer. While they were drying I went out to the garage and
burrowed around, trying to find the ancient suitcase I had brought
from what used to be my home. I looked for fifteen minutes before
I recalled that I had lent it to one of my students who had needed
something disreputable for a prop in a play. *Death of a Salesman*, as
I recalled.

The plan I had evolved during the quiet watches of the night was
simple. It didn't require a lot of fancy clothing, and I had decided to
take relatively few items with me. The remainder could stay in the
cartons in Emile's garage until such time as either I should send for
them, or he decided to use the garage for sheltering his car, which
had wintered quite successfully on the driveway for several years.

Since I couldn't find a suitcase, I returned to the house. By now
Emile was up and clattering about the kitchen. It was about nine or
so.

"I've made a plan," I said to Emile.

He beamed at me. "The schools, *non?*"

"No. Not the schools. I'm through with teaching."

"What then?" asked Emile, his mouth gaping a bit and his tone bordering on incredulous.

"I am going West," I announced quietly. "I am going to go on a retreat from the world for a bit. I'm going to go to California. There I am going to get a job."

"There are no jobs in California," Emile said triumphantly. "I was just reading about it in the paper."

"Of course there are jobs," I said, a bit impatiently. "There are almost thirty million people in California. Don't you think some of them are working?"

Emile was not to be deterred. "But of course some of them are working. Many of them are working, I am sure. But many are not working. And no one who is working will be willing to quit his job so that you can take it. Of that I am quite sure."

I gave up. I could see that Emile's past quarter century of mostly subterranean existence had rendered him as innocent as a lamb about practical matters. I simply said, "I will drive to California. To some place near the sea. There I will get a job, perhaps as a waiter. I will 'go with the flow,' as the saying goes."

At this point I saw Emile wince. I felt bad at having sprung this expression on him so early in the morning, but continued, "In any case, whatever I do, it will have nothing to do with matters of the intellect. In particular, I won't teach French literature for a while — perhaps not ever again. I am going to vegetate for a year, maybe two. I'll live in a shack somewhere. Near the sea. Perhaps while waiting on tables I will meet a woman who is also waiting on table, with whom I can share my life. Perhaps not. In any event I am leaving Indiana. I am too young to die in Indiana."

I could see that my last line had left him perplexed, and the truth was that I didn't really know myself why I had suddenly switched from waiting on table by the sea to waiting for death in a land-locked state. It just seemed the right thing to say at the time. I know that if any one of my young protegées, if that is the word, had heard me declaim that line, she would have been out of her panties and into my bed (the bed I had made of the couch in Emile's den) in a thrice. I had tested similar lines in the past and they seemed to work every time.

Emile was not a French lit groupie, however, and of course I was grateful this was so. He merely said, "A cup of coffee?"

After I had drunk two cups of Emile's coffee, I scared up an old duffle bag. In it I stuffed my clothes and a shaving kit.

"Are you taking no suit?" said Emile. "You cannot present yourself for a position in those things," as he indicated the bag and its contents with a Gallic gesture of contempt.

"Emile," I said gently. "California is not Indiana. People are very casual there. If I show up in a suit to apply for a waiter's job, I will have no hope of getting it. None."

"I hope you are right, *mon vieux*," said Emile somewhat mournfully, as if decrying the standards of dress to which both I and California had sunk. And that was really rather amusing, because a midwestern college French department is not a place where one finds much in the way of elegant attire.

My departure called for a drink, of course, and Emile rummaged around under the sink where normally one keeps caustic solutions for clearing drains, and other such household essentials. He pulled out a bottle of Armagnac. We sat at the breakfast table and drank to each other's health.

"I thank you, Emile, for your helping hand," I said solemnly, and I meant every word. "You are a true friend, and I shall never forget you."

"We will see us again," replied Emile. I noticed that his syntax was slipping under the stress of my departure and rose from the table. He accompanied me to the car, which seemed to be straining at the bit on this fine June morning. I checked once more to make sure that I had my wallet. The back of the car was crammed with stuff. The front passenger seat had a shopping bag with potato chips, some apples, a couple of rolls of breath sweeteners and some other necessaries in it. On the floor was an old Rand McNally road atlas. It was five or six years out of date, but I was quite sure that, with the sorry economic state of the country, few new roads had been built recently between Terre Haute and California.

I got into the car and started the engine, then turned it off. Emile, waiting to wave from the sidewalk, called out, "What is it that you have forgotten?"

I climbed out. "It's nothing," I said. "I just think I'll take a last leak in your downstairs john. Just for luck."

# ten

FENELON HAD BEEN living an extremely exiguous existence since coming to Silicon Valley. Of the eight hundred dollars he had earned at the diner in Winnemucca, Nevada, there remained only slightly more than a hundred. He had paid four hundred dollars to rent a room, utilities included, in a house in a fringe area of Menlo Park. The balance of his expenditures was for gas, movies, and food. As he contemplated his finances one evening, sitting in his office, he realized with a jolt that he had been relying more and more upon the two vending machines in the inner room for his sustenance. The thought of living almost exclusively on the saturated fats and sodium that seemed to comprise the bulk of the ingredients of Kachina blue corn chips made him shudder.

Of course, there were always Arthur Smith's paychecks. He had received one about ten days previously, and was pretty sure he could negotiate it by simply opening his own account, endorsing Arthur's check to himself, and depositing it. He had put off any decision on such an action, so long as he could survive on what he had in his pocket, but his pocket was almost empty.

Fenelon became aware that he was thinking about getting a job.

In fact, he was thinking about waiting on table in one of the innumerable eateries that graced the floor of the Valley. He had cleared eight hundred dollars in Winnemucca, Nevada. Could it be any more difficult to earn money in a rich area of Northern California? Of course, it would be hard, holding down two jobs at once. The second job would probably have to be in the evening, and that would shut him off from the one friend he had made in this part of the world. Also, there was always the possibility that someone from DataDrive might come into whatever place he was working in, and recognize him. How could he explain away the fact that he, an authentic software guru, should have to hold down a second job?

It was with these competing thoughts chasing each other around in his head that he turned to C1, whose incomprehensible lines of code had been replaced by a neatly organized graphical user interface. It was thanks to Chatterjee that Fenelon now had his own mail account, and though all the messages he had received to date were either pronunciamentos from HR, or enthusiatic ravings from the fitness club about a new tummy-flattening program, he still was happy realizing that someone was reaching out to him. Fenelon called up the mail program, and saw with excitement that he had a real message. It was from Chatterjee, and it said:

*From:* chatterjee
*To:* asmith@conman
You might want to look into the attached. Chatterjee.

Fenelon saw that at the bottom of the message was a little icon, which was supposed to represent a postman with a mail sack on his shoulder. He moved the cursor onto this figure, clicked twice, and the following message appeared:

I would be very grateful for any leads on a qualified teacher of
French, to work with our thirteen-year old son. Can pay $15-20 per
hour. Probably three hours/wk. Call 415-324-1233. Thank you.
Lois Winfield
loisw@scads.ddrive.com

Fenelon smiled, and reached for the phone. He dialled Chatterjee's number, but there was no reply. He left a message, saying "Thanks for thinking of me. I might enjoy teaching French. But to a thirteen-year old? Maybe I'll just call them and check it out."

Sixty dollars a week wouldn't solve his financial problems, but if he could get four or five such assignments he could survive quite nicely. He looked at his watch. It was seven-thirty. The thirteen-year old was probably doing his homework, or more likely, watching TV. He reached for the phone again.

The woman who answered the phone listened to Fenelon for a moment, and then said "One minute, please. I'll get Mrs. Winfield."

A moment later a clear, business-like voice said, "This is Lois Winfield."

"My name is Fenelon," said Fenelon. "I saw that you're looking for a French tutor."

"Oh," said the woman. "Are you connected with the school?"

"No, I work at a computer company. I saw your notice on E-mail," said Fenelon.

"Then you work for DataDrive!" said the woman in a pleased tone. "I'm so glad. My husband didn't think I'd get any response at all."

"Do you work for the company, too?" asked Fenelon.

The woman laughed. "No, I don't. My husband set me up with an E-mail account so I can send him messages when he's traveling. So you didn't recognize the name? It's not all that common, is it? My husband is the president of DataDrive. I thought I'd try to advertise on E-mail. And it worked! Wait until I tell Kyle. Forgive me, but I didn't get your name."

"Smith," said Fenelon, thinking quickly. "Arthur Smith. I'm in software."

"Well, how is it you can teach French? Are you qualified?"

"I have a doctorate," said Fenelon. "It's in literature, but I've taught French language at all levels."

"Oh, my!" said the woman. "So you decided to switch careers? That must have been a difficult decision. But I suppose economics played a role. How long ago did you make the change?"

"Fairly recently," said Fenelon.

"Well, if you can, come on over tomorrow evening about this time and we'll talk about it. You can meet Wellington, too, and see how well you two can get along."

"Wellington?" said Fenelon.

"Our son."

AND SO THE next evening Fenelon found himself driving through the winding streets of Los Altos Hills, looking for the Winfield home. He had been able to contact Chatterjee late the previous night. Chatterjee was bemused. After a bit he said, "This cannot be bad for you. Having a domestic contact with the Winfield family is what people here would call a career-enhancing move. I strongly recommend you follow through. After all, it is always better to have two strings to your bow."

"What is the first string?" asked Fenelon.

"Why, being a noted software genius, of course! The lovely thing is that no one will ask you about that in the Winfield home. They will only be concerned with how you perform with the second string, and that is your specialty."

"Teaching thirteen-year olds is not a specialty of mine," said Fenelon, with some trepidation.

"Then you will make it one, I am sure. Though I confess I am confused why you have not yet deposited Arthur Smith's check. After all, you are doing his work."

"I am not!" cried Fenelon.

"Please, my friend, do not yell so loudly over the phone," said Chatterjee. "It hurts my ear. If the real Arthur were sitting in your office he would be thinking away, just as you are no doubt doing."

"Well, he'd be thinking of different things," said Fenelon stiffly. "He wouldn't be worried about paying next month's rent."

"I find your scruples admirable," said Chatterjee. "I only wonder how long they will last."

Fenelon found the entrance to the Winfield home at the end of a long private road which was bordered with flowering bushes. The house faced to the west, and the setting sun caused the tall white columns in front of the house to glow with a soft reflected orange. In front of the house were parked a Jaguar convertible and a Range Rover. To the side of the house, and connected to the driveway, was a large garage with five bays, all closed.

Fenelon parked his Chevrolet behind the Range Rover and climbed out, clutching books and a file in his hand. In the file were his teaching schedules for the last two years, and reprints of two of his publications, on which he had managed to smudge the author's name. The books he had purchased that afternoon. Neither of them was specifically designed for thirteen-year olds, but Fenelon liked the balance each of them struck between the learning of grammar and acquiring  practical use of vocabulary. He thought they might do, and in any case, he couldn't show up for a teaching interview without being able to discuss the materials he would use.

As he stood at the front door Fenelon suddenly realized that he was not suitably dressed for the occasion. This was a wealthy neighborhood, and probably there were not too many persons driving around it in ancient cars, wearing black leather jackets with the elbows out. He remembered Emile's concern that he take more formal garb with him to California. Well, it was too late now, he thought, as the door swung open.

There stood a very tall, large, red-faced woman, wearing an apron over some kind of institutional dress, and clutching a potholder in her left hand. From the long look she gave Fenelon it seemed as if she had brought the potholder with her to use in disposing of him.

"Yes?" she said, in a no-nonsense voice.

"I'm the French teacher," said Fenelon. "I'm here to see Mrs. Winfield." And at that moment there came a click of heels and a voice said, "That's all right, Althea. I'll take it from here." The red-faced woman retreated, and Fenelon found himself face to face with a small, pretty woman wearing a khaki pants suit. Her hair was short and dark, and she was immaculately made up, as if she were about to appear in a magazine advertisement for skin care products. She wore a thin gold chain necklace, and a heavy gold bracelet.

"That was Althea," she said. "She's the family watchdog, as well as the cook. I'm Lois Winfield."

Fenelon found himself shaking hands and being led into the house. After he was seated in a comfortable wing chair in a large, teak-panelled den, with Mrs. Winfield seated opposite him behind a desk, and after he had declined refreshments, he said "Can tell me why you need a tutor for your son? I take it he is studying French in school."

Mrs. Winfield sighed. "No, he's not. He goes to a very progressive school, and they started with French in the fourth grade. But something—I don't know—something went wrong. And he's made up his mind that he hates it. Just hates it! It's so stupid, really, because he's a great mimic, and he's very bright. He decided to drop French this year, the first year where they have a choice, you know? They don't really learn anything in the early years, just sing songs and a few simple things like that. But now he's got this great opportunity and it's going to be a disaster. Just because he's got this *thing* about French."

"What is the disaster? I shouldn't think that much could hinge on a thirteen-year old boy's not wanting to learn French."

Mrs. Winfield put her arms on the desk and leaned toward him. "He's been invited to go to France this September. Last year we hosted a boy from Pau—that's a city in France, you know—for three months. It's part of the Hands-Across-the-Waves movement. You must have heard of that?"

"I'm afraid not," said Fenelon.

"Well, it's our best hope for world peace," said Mrs. Winfield.

"There's no doubt about that. You see, if we can get all these young people to start talking together and learning that they're really all the same under the skin, then when they grow up there'll be this respect for one another. And where there's respect, there can be no hatred and no war."

"You don't anticipate we're going to go to war with France?" said Fenelon.

"No, of course not," smiled Mrs. Winfield. "But the principle works for all nations, doesn't it?"

"Why not send him to some place else?" asked Fenelon, who was thinking that everything else had been tried in the Balkans, so why not a thirteen-year old boy from Los Altos Hills?

"Because Jean-Louis has already been here. He was here for three months, and now the idea is we send Wellington to France to live with *his* family."

"How do the two boys get along?" asked Fenelon.

"Wonderfully well," said Mrs. Winfield. "They really became great chums. But Jean-Louis came here already speaking such beautiful English! And we can't just send Wellington off to a foreign country completely unequipped to deal with anything!"

"How does he feel about going?"

"Well, he wants to see Jean-Louis again. But he's not so keen on France. Frankly, I'd welcome any suggestions you might have on how to handle this."

"Well," said Fenelon, "You might start out with a name change. 'Wellington' is still not a very popular name in France."

"Oh," said Mrs. Winfield vaguely. "Well, would you like to meet him?"

"Sure," said Fenelon.

WELLINGTON WINFIELD WORE a very dirty T-shirt and a pair of baggy shorts that hung on his thin frame. He was about five and a half feet tall, and scrawny. He held a basketball in both hands. His mother had left Fenelon with him, and they were both standing on a paved court behind the garage, looking at each other. A basketball hoop and backboard were mounted at regulation height on the roof of the building.

After a long silence the boy turned and launched the basketball toward the hoop. It swished in cleanly. He retrieved the ball and passed it to Fenelon, who hadn't been expecting it and received it in his stomach.

The boy said "Sorry. You wanna try?"

Fenelon had, in fact, played lots of basketball back in Indiana, which was the home of Larry Bird. Every kid played basketball or you got your face rubbed in it at every opportunity. He bounced the ball once or twice, then suddenly dribbled toward Wellington, who stood transfixed as Fenelon bore down on him. Fenelon faked to his left, then turned right, jumped, and made the shot in mid-air, sweeping his arm up and over his head. The ball bounced off the board and went into the net.

Half an hour later Fenelon had to stop, though Wellington was as energetic as ever. "I'm way out of shape," said Fenelon. "Show me some mercy, will you?"

"You're too fat. You gotta watch what you eat."

"Truer words were never spoke," said Fenelon, as he sank to the turf beside the paved court.

"Spoken," corrected the boy, and he made another shot.

"Listen," said Fenelon, "we're not going to get along if you keep trying to correct my English. That's one thing I've never been able to stand."

"Who says we're gonna get along anyway?" said the boy, who did not seem able to stop bouncing the basketball.

"Your mother wants me to help you learn French. How do you feel about it?"

"I'm not very good at languages," said the boy. "I'm a lot better at math and science and stuff."

"Who says you're not good at languages, Wellington," said Fenelon, and then he stopped as the boy ceased bouncing the basketball and looked at him, eyes blazing with wrath.

"Don't call me 'Wellington' ever again!" he said. "Or you'll be sorry."

"You don't like your name?"

"I hate it. How would you like being called by such a stupid name?"

"I wouldn't," admitted Fenelon. "Besides which, it wouldn't go over in France. Not at all."

The boy came over and stood in front of Fenelon, looking down at him. "No kidding? How come?"

"Because an Englishman named Wellington beat the crap out of Napoleon and the French armies. It was almost two hundred years ago. But the French have long memories."

"No kidding!" said the boy, his face lighting up. "Maybe it's not such a bad name after all. For France, I mean."

"What do people call you?"

"They call me Shark," said the boy. "Because of this," and he opened his mouth and pointed with a grubby finger to a broken front tooth. "My mom wants me to get it fixed but I said no way. I've had it for two years. It's a permanent tooth, you know."

"Shark it is," said Fenelon. "Anyway, you can't tell me you're no good at languages. You're already fluent in one of the most complex languages on the planet."

"You mean English?"

"None other," said Fenelon. "English, you know, is a mixture of languages, based on an old German tongue, but with a whole lot of French and other languages mixed up in it. The verbs are extremely challenging for foreigners to learn. And there are more words in English than in any other language. Guess how many?"

"I dunno," said the boy. "Maybe fifty thousand?"

"Over five hundred thousand. Compared to that, French is child's play, with only a hundred thousand or so."

"You've got a weird name," said the boy. "It sounds kind of foreign. How come you told my mom your name was Smith? Are you on the run?" For Fenelon had slipped up for the first time since getting to the Valley, and had introduced himself to this urchin by his correct name during their one-on-one.

"I'm certainly not on the run," said Fenelon. "It's just a convention. I prefer to be known by my real name only to my closest friends. It's a secret to everyone else."

"I understand that," said the boy.

"As for my name being foreign, it is," said Fenelon. "It's the name of a famous Frenchman. He was an archbishop, almost three hundred fifty years ago. He was an ancestor, rediscovered by my grandmother. She was interested in trying to draw our family tree."

"I thought archbishops weren't allowed to have children," said the boy, sitting down.

"I hadn't thought of that, actually," said Fenelon. "Maybe he was sort of a collateral ancestor. I mean, he didn't have to get directly involved, if you see what I mean."

"Do you know any swear words in French?" said the boy.

"Lots," said Fenelon. "All of them, in fact."

"Gee. Jean-Louis wouldn't teach me any. I don't think he really knew any. It wasn't fair, 'cause I taught him every one I know, which is a lot."

"You seem like a smart guy," said Fenelon.

"They say I'm brilliant," said the boy, digging at the dirt with the heel of a sneaker. "That's why my mom is so mad at me about dropping French. She has this thing about French, it's like the best thing you can do, for God's sake. Really stupid!"

"It must feel good, being able to control at least that part of your life," said Fenelon. "Must be fun, too, being able to get your mom all worked up."

The boy looked at him suspiciously. "Are you bullshitting me?" he asked.

"I'm being perfectly sincere," said Fenelon. "When you're thirteen you don't control very much in your life. Decisions are pretty much made for you. So any way you can get at least *some* control has got to feel pretty good."

"Yeah," said the boy. "Can you teach me some really good swear words in French?"

"Not unless you want to go to France to use them," said Fenelon. "Otherwise it'll just be a waste of time and energy. And your family's money."

"How much are they paying you?" asked the boy.

"It hasn't been decided yet," said Fenelon. "First you have to agree to learn French. Then I can negotiate."

"You look kinda poor, so I'd guess they'd give you maybe fifty dollars an hour. My parents don't like to see poverty in the world."

"Well, we'll see," said Fenelon. "The big question is, do you want to tackle French or not?"

"Sure," said the boy. "If you'll teach me those words. And also we gotta play some hoop, otherwise I'll go nuts."

"I'll make you a deal," said Fenelon. "I'll teach you one swear word or expression for each irregular verb you master. I mean, really master, backwards and forwards."

"You mean, good swears?"

"Really ripe ones," said Fenelon. "Of course, this has to be between me and you."

"What's an irregular verb?" said the boy.

"I'll show you," said Fenelon. "Let's find a table and some paper."

TWO WEEKS LATER Fenelon's car wouldn't start. The starter whirred and whirred, but the engine wouldn't catch. Shark was watching him. Finally Fenelon got out of the car. "It's getting old," he said. "Gotta get the EFI checked, I guess."

"*Putain de bagnole,*" said Shark, with a surprisingly good accent.

Fenelon glanced guiltily at the house behind them. "Remember," he cautioned, "you're not supposed to know these things. Can't you wait 'til you get to France?"

"I've gotta practice," said Shark. "Besides, my mom is so happy that I'm getting all this culture, I don't think she'd mind an occasional swear."

"Now I've got to call the triple A and a cab," said Fenelon. "I can't leave this thing here all night."

"My Dad is here," said Shark. "He can give you a ride to wherever you've got to go. And the triple A can pick the car up whenever they get around to it. They're always coming to get the Jag."

And so it was that Fenelon found himself in the Range Rover, seated beside Kyle Winfield, president and CEO of DataDrive, being chauffeured to downtown Mountain View. Now that he was in the money again, Fenelon had taken to eating better, and he was headed for a sushi house on Castro.

"We're pretty pleased with the progress Wellington seems to be making," said Kyle. "He's found some kind of motivation. I mean it! He's got Lois quizzing him every morning over breakfast on those irregular verbs. She says she's learning as much French as he is!"

"Oh, I doubt that," said Fenelon.

"I know you work for the company, but maybe you missed your true calling. My wife says you've got a Ph.D."

"Yes," said Fenelon. "But I'm on a new career now."

"Well, I hope you're enjoying yourself," said Kyle. "You're in software? Which group?"

"In development," said Fenelon. "You can let me off here." They had entered Castro.

Kyle pulled the big Range Rover over to the curb, and Fenelon opened the door and got out. "Thanks a lot," he said, leaning in to grasp Kyle's hand.

Kyle called out to him as Fenelon was about to shut the door. "We're really glad you can come over so often. You're doing a great job. Lois thinks you're a magician, and... well I guess you know how

Wellington feels about you. God, I've gotta stop calling him that, now. He says it's bad for American-French relations. Though how 'Shark' can help improve them I don't know. Anyway, anything I can do for you, you call my admin, Penelope. She controls my calendar."

The Range Rover moved away from the curb, and Fenelon stood there. In his pocket were three crisp twenty-dollar bills, folded once. He was feeling quite content. Chatterjee was due to show up in a few minutes, and Fenelon was going to see if he could induce him to eat raw fish. He was looking forward to it.

As Fenelon moved toward the corner where he was to meet Chatterjee, he didn't notice two figures who had been standing a few feet away, in the mouth of a dark alley. Jerzy Bobochek had consumed five Black Russians and sixteen buffalo wings, while King Salamon had been close behind with four Black Russians, two Mexican beers, and two plates of nachos with extra salsa.

"Jesus, did you see that?" asked Jerzy?

"I saw and heard," said King. "Kyle really likes that guy, whoever he is."

"That was Arthur Smith," said Jerzy.

King put his arm around Jerzy's shoulder. "Well, ol' buddy, if I were you I'd treat him very, very well. Kyle doesn't get personally close to lots of people, but the whole family seems to have taken Arthur to its bosom. Me, I'm glad I'm in hardware. I'm gonna stay out of the guy's way."

# eleven

"So you see," said Chatterjee, chewing on a twig, "that is the story of the Ramayana. It is the basis of much of the culture of Southern Asia."

"It is a wonderful story," said Fenelon. "But I don't think the ending would appeal to the modern woman."

They were sitting on a log a few feet off Route 35. It was late afternoon the Saturday following the dinner at the Silk Saree.

"You mean the part about Rama putting Sita to the test?" asked Chatterjee. "Yes, he was not willing to accept her word that she had not slept with the evil Rawana. Or maybe he did believe her, and put her to the test as a political gesture. So that there could never be any bad rumor about her."

"Still," said Fenelon, "having her walk through a roaring fire was a little harsh for a political gesture."

"I agree," said Chatterjee. "Unless, of course, he knew that she was innocent and so would not be harmed."

Fenelon sighed. He gazed out over the hillside at the Pacific two or three miles away. It was getting hazy. "You know a lot," he said. "Where did you have the time to learn all this stuff? You know lots about culture and literature, but you still had time to learn all about computers."

"And management," said Chattejee. "I studied management after I learned about computers. I was admitted to the Indian Institute of Management in Ahmadabad. It's a city in Gujarat. Being admitted there was quite an honor for me. Young men and women from all over India apply to this school, but only a very few are admitted each year."

"Well, from the management point of view, what do you think of our division?" asked Fenelon.

"Bobochek is quite ignorant, of course. He is one of those persons of whom it can rightly be asked how they can possibly have arrived at the positions they hold. One asks whether those who appoint them to these posts of power are themselves ignorant, or whether there is some subtle interplay of politics and psychology that causes a temporary suspension of the rational faculties."

Fenelon was impressed. "Of course, there must be stupid people in every company, in every industry."

"This is undoubtedly true," said Chatterjee. He turned his slight and twisted body toward Fenelon, and bobbed his head slowly for emphasis. "But it is disturbing to see it in high technology. Egomaniacs, the power-hungry, the fumblers—let them infest the soap powder companies where they can do no harm. The waste of time and energy and resources in high technology because of the need to go around or through the Bobocheks is enormous."

"Perhaps you should run the division," Fenelon said, smiling. But to his dismay he saw that Chatterjee was scowling at him.

"You think this is a joke," said Chatterjee. "But I assure you, Fenelon, that I could run the division very very well indeed, and infinitely better than Mr. Jerzy Bobochek. I have the brains, and I have the ability to deal effectively with people. And I assure you, despite the way I look, I can be very tough when it is necessary."

Fenelon had been slouching forward, but now he sat straight up. This was the first allusion Chatterjee had made to his physical condition. "Chatterjee, I am damn sure you are right," he said. "Please believe me. I was only smiling just now because I don't think there's any chance of your ever running the division."

"You are correct, my friend," said Chatterjee, and the scowl disappeared. "There is no chance of my being a divisional vice-president, at least not at this company. Not even if I am successful in launching Nemo. They will give me a bonus check, which will be very nice, and I will get a certificate. And I will get to make some brief remarks at the company meeting at the end of the year. That is all. But for the moment I am not ambitious for myself. I have what I want."

"And what is that?" asked Fenelon.

"I have a very nice home in Fremont, and a very nice sister who takes care of it. An interesting assignment at work, and some very smart engineers to work with. And a friend."

Fenelon was afraid to ask whether this friend was a man or a woman. It did not seem likely that a tiny cripple from the Indian subcontinent would have a girlfriend, but one could not be sure. He did not want to risk offering offense. So he said nothing.

"My friend," said Chatterjee, "is, of course, you. You are a very interesting person to me, but that interest is not what constitutes friendship. I call you my friend, first because you trusted me with the secret that you were not Arthur Smith. I find it irresistible to be trusted. Second, you are an adventurer. You got into your automobile and drove away from what was familiar, and toward the unfamiliar."

"Unfamiliar is right," said Fenelon.

"I find it amazing, though, that you somehow managed to reach the age of... how old did you say you were?"

"Thirty-nine," said Fenelon.

"Thirty-nine. You managed to reach this fairly advanced age without ever having tasted Indian food. Yet at my cousin's restaurant, after I managed to stop your stream of inquiries, you dutifully ate everything in sight. Even the curried sheep's brains."

"Curried sheep's brains?" said Fenelon.

"Many Americans find them too spicy," said Chatterjee.

"Ah-h," said Fenelon.

"But it is getting late, my friend. We came up here to discuss how to resolve two problems, and we have made little headway with either of them. The first, and if you will excuse me, the more important of the two, is my problem, which is Nemo. Second is your problem, which is how to avoid prosecution and possible imprisonment for impersonating another man, and pocketing money which is rightfully his."

"I could just disappear," said Fenelon. "No one knows who I am. I could just drive down the coast and live somewhere."

"Where, for example?" asked Chatterjee.

"Well, I could get some sort of job, and maybe buy a shack somewhere. I don't know. I've never been down the coast."

"Do you happen to have several hundred thousand dollars at your disposal?" Chatterjee had screwed his head around and was peering up into Fenelon's face with a grin.

"Of course not," retorted Fenelon.

"Then I am afraid the shack is out of the picture. Shacks on the California coast cost a great deal of money these days. Cannery Row has become Park Place. Or Boardwalk."

"Do you play Monopoly?" asked Fenelon, intrigued by this allusion.

"Indeed," said Chatterjee. "I used to be very good at it when I was a child. We had two sets, and my sisters and I used to combine the money into one big bank. I usually played the banker. It was fun, handling all the bills, even though one knew, of course, that it was not real money."

"Of course. So what do I do?"

"That will work itself out after we solve my problem," Chatterjee said, laughing. "I am sure that you and I have the wit and daring to outsmart the management of DataDrive, the Mountain View Police, and the FBI."

"The FBI?" Fenelon said nervously.

"First, Nemo. Then we will tackle the FBI."

"Nemo is simple," said Fenelon. "You need to consult with someone who is just as smart as you are in software development, but who hasn't been as close to the project. Maybe someone who hasn't had anything at all to do with the project."

"There are few people who are as smart as I am in the area of development. I know it sounds very conceited, but it is the truth. There are consultants, of course, but I have no budget for that, and besides, I am not sanguine about the likelihood of getting someone really good. There is a small firm I know of in Palo Alto, but at present they are working on a major project in Japan."

"I know someone you could get," Fenelon said.

"Then please tell."

"Well," said Fenelon, "there's always Arthur Smith. You tried to consult with him already, only he was me, so it didn't work out. But if I had been him, or rather if he had been at DataDrive where he should have been and I had been waiting on table in Santa Cruz, or perhaps Capitola, you could have consulted to your heart's content. For free, too."

"I wish you would not refer so much to your desire to be a café waiter," said Chatterjee. "You were not cut out to be a waiter, and I do not think you would be successful at it."

"Christ!" swore Fenelon. "If I can't be successful at being a waiter, then I'm good for nothing!" And then, because it made him feel better, he repeated "Nothing!"

"That too will have to be seen. Right now you are being extremely useful to me, since you have called my attention to the obvious solution to my problem. The obvious is sometimes the most difficult to see. We must find Arthur Smith as soon as possible, and install him in his office."

Fenelon said nothing.

"Let us start Monday morning," said Chatterjee.

"Listen," Fenelon said, nervously. "I agree the answer to your problem is to find this guy. But what if he's not findable? What if he's had an accident of some kind? Gone over a cliff, or been eaten by a shark? When I told you I wasn't Arthur Smith your first comment was something to the effect that I must have killed him. What if the police think that?"

"The police must not know that we are looking for him," said Chatterjee. "Come, help me pick up these bags. They are beginning to blow around in the wind."

It was true. Surrounding the large log on which they were both perched were several empty Kachina bags, as well as a quantity of empty plastic juice containers. Sliding down from the log, Fenelon began chasing the bags. He collected them one by one.

"I have all the bottles," Chatterjee said, hopping toward Fenelon, his large hands encasing seven or eight of them. "Where is the trash bag?"

THEY WERE IN Fenelon's car, heading back down to the valley. "This is a very nice car, Fenelon," said Chatterjee. "It is old, but it would be worth a lot of money in India."

Fenelon was silent.

"I sense that you are bothered. Please tell what is on your mind."

"How are we going to find Arthur Smith without going to the police?" asked Fenelon. "I don't have the money to hire a detective."

"Indeed you do," said Chatterjee. "You have all of Arthur Smith's money. And if it is not justified to use a man's own money to find him when he is missing, then I do not see what is. But that will not be necessary. We will find out everything about Arthur Smith that we can from internal sources. Then we will track him down."

"Internal sources? What internal sources? Who knows anything at all about Arthur Smith at DataDrive? And we can't go to his old company. They'd never even let us inside."

"By internal sources I mean Ms. Toni Hunter," said Chatterjee.

"Toni? She doesn't know anything about Arthur! She thinks *I'm*

Arthur. What can she...?" But Fenelon was silenced by the sight of Chatterjee's waving both hands over his head. He was so short that he could do this almost without touching the roof of the Chevy. Fenelon knew that Chatterjee made these gestures only when he was very excited or upset, so he waited.

"Toni knows, or has in her control, all the information we need about Arthur. I remember well, when I joined DataDrive myself, that I was required to give all sorts of information about my family, for example. It must be presumed that, barring a personal tragedy of immense dimensions, Arthur, too, has a family. I would suggest that we start with the family. Who, for example, is his beneficiary on his insurance policy? Do you recall?"

"No, I don't. Why should I?" said Fenelon, irritated. "I signed a bunch of papers that the admin gave me. She told me that she had got all the information from some recruiter, who got it from me. I mean, from Arthur, of course."

"So you do not remember. That does not matter. The point is, the information is there."

"The admin would lose her job if she showed it to you," said Fenelon. "And she'd think I was nuts if I asked her for it."

"Don't you have a copy of your policy application?"

"No," admitted Fenelon. "I don't think I took anything. I think Daphne has it all."

"The personnel folders are kept in a locked file cabinet in Toni's office," said Chatterjee. "Please watch out for the stop signs. We are out of the hills now, and you drove through the last sign without stopping. The folders will be sent over to the corporate files at the end of the quarter, which is ten days away. But we should start right away. I will get the information from Toni tomorrow. Then you can find Arthur. I cannot take any time off now, because of Nemo. But no one will miss you."

"Thanks," said Fenelon. "But Toni will never give you access to my files." He could conjure the picture of a diminutive Ranjan Chatterjee being driven from Toni's door by a withering look and one or two well-placed sarcastic phrases; it was an image he did not relish in the least. "I think I should talk to Toni. If need be, I will confess the whole thing to her."

"You needn't," said Chatterjee. "I will tell her myself. I am better equipped to handle her reaction."

Fenelon laughed.

"I am quite serious," Chatterjee said.

"I will bet you a hundred dollars that Toni will never give you my files," Fenelon said.

"For someone making as much as Arthur Smith you may well bet such a small sum," said Chatterjee. "Pull the car over here, please."

They were just crossing El Camino, and Fenelon stopped in front of a Mexican restaurant. "Why are we stopping?" he said. "I'll run you home."

"I will bet you ten thousand dollars that Toni will not only provide me with your files, but she will hand carry them to my office."

Fenelon was silent. This was one of the most surprising and, Fenelon had to admit, delightful persons he had ever met in his whole life. "OK, Mr. Chatterjee. I won't bet with you, because you know something you're not telling. What have you got on Toni Hunter?"

Chatterjee said blandly "What makes you think I have something on Ms. Hunter?"

"Because she can be one tough bitch, that's why! Because she has no patience with anyone who doesn't either hump her or promote her, preferably both. That's why."

"It is true that Toni is consumed with becoming the director for recruiting. For some strange reason she has made this the goal of her life, although as we discussed earlier today life itself is ephemeral. Tomorrow morning at about nine o'clock she will learn from me that her promotion depends on her cooperating to the fullest with our quest for the true Arthur Smith."

"Because..." prompted Fenelon.

"Because, my friend, if she does not I shall mail copies of these to every officer of the company." And so saying, Chatterjee pulled from his leather jacket an envelope and handed it to Fenelon, who opened it and inspected the contents wordlessly.

He was looking at color photos, some of which were blurry from camera shake, some of which were out of focus, and at least two of which clearly showed himself and Toni Hunter naked and entwined on a futon. Behind the futon rose two dark vending machines, like immense graven images supervising fertility rites. Carmelita had not had much experience as a pornographer, but as a candid photographer she was definitely showing promise.

# twelve

SAMMI BOYADJIAN HAD not been born in Brooklyn, nor in any of the other four boroughs of the City of New York. Instead he had been born in Paterson, New Jersey, in his uncle's house. His maternal aunt had been a midwife in Sarikamis, in eastern Turkey, and it was she who had assisted her sister in bringing Sammi into the world.

Since Sammi was the first male born into the Boyadjian clan in America there was pressure brought to bear to keep him in Paterson, as a sort of living trophy. His aunt and uncle also wanted to watch over the little child's upbringing. But grateful though Sammi's mother was to her sister for all that she had done, she nevertheless felt that it would be better if she returned to the apartment in Brooklyn, which was in a good neighborhood with several Armenian families, and not too far from Prospect Park. Sammi's father, who had rapidly tired of the commute on public transportation between Brooklyn and Paterson, was very grateful for this decision.

Sammi's father ran a small business selling Oriental rugs. His business occupied the front corner of a furniture store six blocks from the Boyadjian apartment, and one of Sammi's earliest memories was of himself and his friend Nick Falotti, who lived one floor down, rolling around and turning somersaults on top of a stack of carpets, to the amusement of passersby on the other side of the show window. His father was a quiet, tolerant man, of slight build and unprepossessing manner. But he knew his carpets and the business did all right.

Sammi went to public schools, which were better in those days, and at one point of his life dreamed of going to Columbia. But that wasn't to be. For one thing, his two sisters arrived three and four years after him, and money was scarce. He ended up at Queens College, which was a lot cheaper.

When he turned twelve, Sammi started working with his father Saturdays and some evenings. Mostly what he did was move, roll and wrap carpets. If a customer decided that he or she wanted a rug that was fifteen down in the stack, all the rugs on top had to be removed so that a final decision could be made based on the total impression, rather than just a corner. It was muscle-building work, and Sammi, who was stocky and strong, got pretty good at it. In high school he went out for wrestling and made the team. In his junior year he made it to the state semi-finals, and in his senior year he was the champ in his weight class.

That same year, Sammi's younger sister, Mayna, was taking ballet, and had to go pretty far by bus each Tuesday and Thursday evening. One of the defining episodes in Sammi's life began the night he returned from wrestling practice and found the family in the kitchen. His mother and the middle sister, Irene, were crying; his father was pale, and Mayna was sitting at the table holding a towel with ice in it to the side of her head.

"What's going on?" Sammi had said.

"Mayna had some trouble on Bedford Avenue," said his father gruffly.

"You mean, someone beat her up?"

Sammi's mother had stopped crying. "Some man tried to drag your sister into a car," she said. "God, I don't know what the world is coming to."

It took a while to get the whole story. Someone had pulled over to ask Mayna directions to somewhere, but as soon as she had come over to the curb a man jumped out on the passenger side and tried to push her in. There was no one nearby, but Mayna had screamed and fought, hitting her head on the edge of the open door. She had blacked out for a moment, but, thank God, a bus went past just then and the driver had pulled over, smashing right into the car. The two men had run away. The police had come and taken Mayna to the station, from where she had called home. They were trying to track down the occupants of the car.

For a couple of weeks after the attack Mayna refused to leave the apartment, even though her friends stopped by to walk her to school. She didn't even want to see Nick during this time, though nothing really bad had happened to her. Nick, Sammi's friend since they were little, had been going with Mayna for a year or so, even though Mrs. Boyadjian thought that Mayna, at fifteen, was too young. Also, Nick had dropped out of school two years ago, at sixteen, had moved away from home, and was working somewhere in the Falotti family businesses, which Mrs. Boyadjian suspected were connected with the Mafia.

"Son of a bitch," was Nick's initial reaction to the news.

Sammi said "She's OK, except she doesn't want anyone to see her face. It looks a little like the full moon, at the moment. Also, she's gonna have a scar."

"Shit," said Nick. "She'll see me." But she wouldn't, not for days.

"Nick, stop sending flowers, for Christ sake," said Sammi. They were having Cokes in a social club owned by Nick's family. "The girl's not dying. She's fine, I tell ya. My mom thinks something major is going on between you two, all those flowers."

"Well, let her think what she wants," said Nick.

"Mayna's scared those guys are waiting to get her," said Sammi.

"That's why she doesn't wanna leave the apartment. The police aren't getting anywhere trying to find them."

Nick was thoughtful. He had a rather narrow, Rudolf Valentino kind of face which was spoiled just a bit by a broken nose that hadn't healed right. He was quiet for so long that Sammi got impatient and flipped his wadded-up straw cover in Nick's face.

"C'mon, I gotta go," he said.

Nick said "Sammi, I'm gonna tell you something, and you're gonna tell Mayna. But you gotta swear on your mother's life you'll never tell anyone else."

"Sure," said Sammi.

"No, I mean it," said Nick. "I'll get in a lotta trouble if it gets out I told you. I was gonna tell Mayna, yeah, but shit, I can't get to see her. So I gotta go through you."

"OK, I swear. You know I can keep a secret, Nicky. Remember the candy boxes from the truck?"

Nick laughed. "OK, listen to me. What would you do to those guys if you had them right here, right now?"

"You mean the guys that tried to get Mayna?"

Nick snorted. "Naw, I mean the guys that sell hotdogs at Shea. Who else you think I mean?"

"I guess I'd keep 'em here and call the cops," said Sammi.

"No kidding?" said Nick. "That's not what I'd do. But anyway, it doesn't matter, 'cause they're not likely to show for a while."

Sammi looked at Nick, who grinned at him.

"What happened?" said Sammi.

"Well," said Nick, "one of those guys is over at Riker's right now." Riker's Island was the prison in Flushing Bay. "Course, the cops don't know he's the guy was driving the car that night. They think he held up a liquor store five, six weeks ago. But me, I know he was driving the car. I want you to tell your sister that guy's never gonna hurt nobody again."

"He's in for a stretch?" said Sammi.

"He'll be out of there and up to Ossining in a few weeks," said

Nick. "As soon as he gets out of the hospital. That fucker's never gonna drive a car again, either. Seems he had an accident last week. Slipped and fell in the cell block. Both his arms broke in lotsa places."

"Holy shit," said Sammi.

"You don't tell Mayna that part," said Nick. "Just tell her the guy's in the slammer, gonna stay there for a long, long time. Tell her I said so. She'll believe you."

Sammi was silent, so Nick said "The other guy, the guy that grabbed her, I can't tell you what happened to him. I know but I can't tell you. Just tell Mayna she's got nothing to be afraid of from either of those guys. Tell her I wanna see her. Please, Sammi, you do that for me."

Sammi got Nick's message to Mayna, and she saw Nick the next day. Mrs. Boyadjian knew that Nick had sent a message to Mayna through her son, and though she didn't know what it was, she was so glad that her daughter had rejoined the world that she welcomed Nick with open arms.

Sammi had thought about this for years. For all that he had grown up on the streets, he was a peaceful young man, and hated the violence that seemed to be growing around the neighborhood. He didn't at all like to think that human beings were capable of causing intense suffering to others. Yet, in a way, he was ashamed of himself for not having sought out Mayna's attackers, wreaking vengeance on them. He had relied on the forces of law and order. Should he have done more? And after all, what could he have done? He had no idea how one could track down two anonymous men in a huge city. Still, Nick, or someone he knew, had managed to do it.

One positive thing that did come out of all this was that Sammi developed an awareness of how vulnerable people were. Especially women.

It was a couple of days after Chatterjee had shown Fenelon the photos that Sammi Boyadjian decided to invite the new software guru to lunch. He figured it was another way he would really be able to get the straight poop on what was happening in Jerzy's area. New impressions generally reflect truth, Sammi knew, and Arthur Smith's observations about his environment could give Sammi some ammunition to use in a little campaign he had been planning for some time now. And so it was that Sammi took Fenelon in his new Porsche over to The Stilton Cheese, which was the closest thing to a business executives' lunch club anywhere on the Peninsula. Fenelon was delighted to find fried calamari on the menu. For his part, Sammi decided to take the lean route and ordered the grilled mahi-mahi special. They each had a small bottle of Calistoga fizzy water, plain, and Sammi ordered a double Scotch on ice.

The Stilton Cheese was expensive. It had a view over the Bay, and was located toward the end of the glide path of planes landing at SFO. Fenelon was intrigued by the constant procession of aircraft, each with its brightly colored logo on the tail. Lufthansa, British Air, China Airlines, QANTAS, Reno Air.

Fenelon found himself wishing he were booked on the return flight of any one of those planes. Life had gotten so complicated it was getting hard to sort it all out. The previous Sunday he had visited a farmers market in a town by the sea. Strolling from booth to booth he inspected the vegetables, and bought a blueberry muffin and an apple for his breakfast. The produce was sold by the farm families that had raised it, and Fenelon had realized, as he looked at these brown-skinned working people that there was a whole life outside academe and high tech. Perhaps he could retire quietly to a farm, and learn to grow things like Brussels sprouts, or artichokes. They were, he had heard, excellent cash crops.

Suddenly Fenelon realized that Sammi had stopped talking and seemed to be waiting for a reply.

"I'm sorry," he said. "I was just thinking."

"I could tell, said Sammi. "You seemed preoccupied. I have lots of respect for you techies. You're always thinking. I just asked you how things were going in the labs. Got a decent assignment yet? If you don't, let me know. I'll tell you the truth, just between us. Landing you was quite a coup for me, and I want you to be happy so that you can help us push the envelope."

"Yes, I see," said Fenelon, to whom this metaphor meant nothing.

"Again between us, Jerzy Bobochek makes a lot of noise, but he's really just an empty suit. I won't say anything more, but there's gonna be some changes made in the near future."

"You mean changes affecting Jerzy?" asked Fenelon.

"You said it! That guy is a menace. But up to now he's always made his numbers and his MBOs, and in this industry you could be Attila the Hun, raping and pillaging, and still get the Boy Scout of the Week award, just as long as the performance was there."

"Even if the long-term effect on the company is bad?"

Sammi smiled grimly. "Look, Arthur, you've been up to your eyeballs in the science side of this thing, but I've been down in the business muck. 'Long-term?' There is no long term in this industry. If Jerzy can rig things so he just gets through the quarter OK, he's a hero, even if all of us know that the whole goddam company will come crashing down the day after the books close."

"Well, maybe if he does well this quarter he'll be promoted out of where he is," said Fenelon.

"You're getting my drift," said Sammi with a grin. "He'd really like to have my job. But I don't plan to retire for a while yet. There are three sure ways to get a promotion in high tech. The first is to switch companies. That's what the ordinary good performers do. They can't make it where they are, because they're too busy doing a good job to work the system like you have to.

"The second way is to politick, pull strings, call in markers, scheme, window-dress whatever it is you're doing, and move quick when you see the chance. And the third way is to screw up so bad that they gotta move you out of there. If you're a little guy they can just fire your ass, of course, though it may take a few months because HR's gotta construct a case that'll stand up in court. In case the guy tries to get tough. When you get to Jerzy's level, though, the way they do it is they promote you, so you can't bitch publicly because you'd look stupid. Like they make you the president of some little no-account sub that's never gonna get any significant funding. Or they send you overseas."

"Overseas?" said Fenelon.

"Just watch," said Sammi.

The main courses arrived and for a while the two men ate in silence. After a bit Fenelon put down his fork and said, "What did you mean about 'window-dressing' a few minutes ago?"

"I dunno," said Sammi. "What did I say?"

"You said that you've got to window-dress what you're doing, to get promoted. You mean, to get the higher-ups to notice you?"

"I'll give you a real-life example," said Sammi. "About eight years ago, only believe me, the same thing happens today, I was in hardware. A guy I knew was running a marketing group. This was in another company. We had a number of new programs we were getting started, so we needed some firepower. This guy, he didn't report to me but I knew what was going on. He had ten people reporting to him. That was pretty impressive, because he was only twenty-nine and like me, he didn't have a real good education. No MBA, right? Well, we had these programs going along pretty good after a while, and this guy got some kudos and he started to look around.

"Now it takes time to get a new job in one of these companies, even with a good track record, 'cause you wanna be sure always to get a promotion; and after you get to a certain level these are kinda hard to come by. So this guy was looking and talking to people. But in the meantime, his group had done most of the hard work launching these programs, see, and now the workload was way down. Really, there was work for maybe, like four or five people. But he had these ten. Sure enough, I find out that one or two of his people come to him, saying 'we don't have enough to do.' You get some like that in this industry.

"So to keep them happy this guy takes some of the workload away from the others and piles it on these two, who go away happy. The others are happy too, because they've got more time to spare to spend with their families, or whatever. They're not overworked, see?

"Now, from the company point of view, this is a big waste of resources, because some of the other functions, they're screaming for headcount. And they can't get it."

"Why didn't he let some of his people go to those other jobs?" asked Fenelon.

"That's the point, Arthur! If he had done that, his chances for promotion would've gone way down. Because his job would have lost some of its importance. The more people you got reporting to you, the more important you look. No matter if it's real or not. Yeah, it's crazy, I know. But in a few months this guy was outta there, made director of channels business. A great job."

"What happened to his group?" Fenelon said.

"It was gone within two months after he left it. They kept a couple guys on to maintain the programs. The others they gave two months to find new jobs in the company."

"Did they get them?"

"I dunno. Two months seems like a lot of time, but you'd be surprised how fast it goes by. Of course, those guys weren't insisting on any kind of promotion, or anything like that. They just wanted to keep the cash flow going, so they could pay the mortgage."

At this point the waiter appeared pushing a dessert cart. Fenelon was full of calamari, and had, besides, an unsettled feeling in the pit of his stomach. "I'll pass," he said.

Sammi said "I'll take that cake, and put some raspberry sauce on it please."

After the waiter had withdrawn, Sammi said "You know, Arthur, you're probably wondering why I'm saying all these things. I meant to find out how things are with you and in the labs, and I'm giving you a lecture on practical business."

"Well things are really OK with me. I guess the morale isn't too high in the labs, though, from what I hear."

"Is that so?" said Sammi.

Fenelon realized with a jolt that it might appear as if he had taken sides in an internecine skirmish. "I don't mean to say anything about Jerzy," he said hastily.

"I understand," said Sammi. "Has Jerzy been to visit you yet?"

"No."

"Very interesting," said Sammi. "You are the best thing that ever happened to that guy and he doesn't realize it. Hasn't paid you even a courtesy call?"

"Not yet."

"Well, he'd better do it soon," said Sammi. "If he's ever gonna get to do it at all."

# thirteen

**K**ING HAD A unique way about him, that was for sure. Albie, the admin for the hardware marketing group, was chatting about it over the phone with Frank, who worked at a small applications firm a couple of miles away, and who was his particular friend. Albie knew that Frank had a crush on him. Albie didn't like to play games, he wasn't that sort. But the problem was, though he really liked Frank a lot, he just didn't know how he really felt about getting into another relationship at this time. It was only three months since he and Roman had split up, and the pain was still very much with him. The therapy had helped a lot, and Albie felt he was just getting back onto level ground again. To make himself vulnerable right now, no, he couldn't do it. He had to heal first.

But it was very pleasant to talk to Frank, either over coffee at his favorite local hangout, or by phone as he was doing now. Albie didn't know about Security's eavesdropping operation, but in any case he wouldn't have cared. He didn't spend lots of time talking to Frank or anyone else other than business people, and since he was supporting about forty people, unbelievable though that may sound, he felt he earned the right to a few minutes of phone time now and then. He was perfectly prepared to go to the mat with

Security, or his manager, or even King Salamon himself, who was two layers up from his manager. The funny thing was that of all the people in the division, Albie was the one person King wouldn't dare confront, for the simple reason that Albie was a Level Four admin, hardworking, and popular with all the folks he supported and with the other admins. If King had ever cracked the whip at Albie it could have ended with a revolt of the admins, who were in general tired of being, at least in their own eyes, overworked and underpaid. And a revolt of the admins would quickly bring DataDrive to its knees.

Today, Albie had been listening with sympathy as Frank described how unbearable the situation had become in the apartment he shared with three other young men in the Haight. Frank made the commute down the Peninsula every day because he was from out of state, had only been in California for a few months, and had naturally ended up in the Haight where he thought he could find a supportive environment.

"But it's not!" he complained to Albie. "It's turned into three against one, and all because of the Green-Eyed Monster. Terry and Mikos are an item, of course, and Jamie brings this Jamaican sweetie home with him last Saturday and he sees me and ignores Jamie completely! He dances with me the whole night! Nothing serious, I mean I'm attracted to him, of course. Who wouldn't be... that accent, those curls! And muscles, like everywhere. A good dancer, too. But I didn't start it, he did! The Jamaican, I mean. Nothing happened, though that wasn't Rex's—that's his name— fault. He tried, but I am not someone's casual lay. But no matter, for five days now I've been frozen out, just frozen!"

Albie thought he could see which way this was heading. He had a great little pad in Palo Alto, sort of a carriage house hiding behind one of the big houses in a street off Hamilton. He was actually buying this place, swinging the down payment with his share of the money from his aunt's estate, and with his dad in Little Rock guaranteeing the mortgage. It was Albie's family's way of making sure that he stayed in California. Not that they didn't love him, because they did. It was just better for everyone if he didn't drop in too often, back in Arkansas.

One night, a few weeks ago, CalTrain had stopped running for a few hours, because of an unfortunate encounter between one of its locomotives and a momentarily bewildered pedestrian attempting to walk to El Camino at a grade crossing in Menlo Park. Frank hadn't been able to get home, and had called Albie, who had invited him to his place for a stir-fry dinner. They had had a good time just chatting, and Albie saw that Frank was impressed by the little house. Most of his friends were similarly impressed, and some of them had said outright that they would like to move in, relationship or no. But though it would have helped a lot with the mortgage, which was killing Albie, he couldn't let anyone into his life, even in a peripheral sense, just now. Not until the ghost of Roman had been exorcised.

The thing was that Frank didn't even know about Roman yet, and Albie couldn't figure out why he hadn't told him. So when he sensed that Frank was manoeuvring around the housing issue he felt a need to change the topic, and this he did.

"Roommates can be really unreasonable," he said. "And after a hard day at work, who needs more aggro? Which reminds me, what's the status of your promotion? Any word?" Frank had been bucking for an in-grade promotion, which really meant  more money.

"Nothing, *nada*," came Frank's voice over the wire. "It's hurry up and wait. And if I have to move out, I'll need the extra dough. What's new on your end?"

"Remember I told you the Facilities people were in here to resite offices?" said Albie. "With the downsizing we're taking in the whole marcom group on this floor. They've lost six people, and Facilities thinks it can save a few pennies by squeezing them in here. Of course, to do this they've got to move partitions and even take out some of the closed offices. You know what that means!"

In DataDrive most of the employees occupied partitioned cubicles, until you got to the director level and above. Of course, all the HR managers had closed offices, because they occasionally had to have difficult conversations with people, conversations best kept private. But otherwise a closed office was a distinct mark of rank.

"The butterfly!" giggled Frank. It was his private way of referring to King Salamon, whose fame was legendary among a small group of Albie's close associates. Frank was referring to the Monarch butterfly. A King was a monarch, and hence his clever use of the term.

"None other," said Albie. "He's had this choice corner office, overlooks the pond, since he got here. But we've now got eight directors on the first floor, and only six closed offices. So what Facilities decided to do was knock out all but two of the offices, because that's the only way they can fit the marcom people in. They had a drawing, you know, to see who would get the offices. Only it was Facilities who did the drawing, the directors weren't there. They did it at seven in the morning, yesterday. Put all eight names in a wastebasket, pulled out two. Posted the results on the board."

"And the butterfly?" said Frank.

"Stayed in the wastebasket, I'm afraid."

Frank laughed. "Bet he was pleased when he came in."

Albie said "You have but *no idea*! He was *pissed*! But the funniest thing is, he's refusing to move! They had arranged a big cubicle for him, not a bad place, and after all it's only temporary. In a few months we're all going to be in the new HQ building. But yesterday, two guys show up with cartons, going to pack and move his stuff, and he stands in the door and throws a fit! It was one of these scenes, like 'over my dead body!' Dramatic! So now we've got five directors moved very peacefully, and one is in his corner office, and one is waiting to get into King's office, and King is vowing death and dismemberment to whoever crosses his threshold!"

"What *is* it with that man?" asked Frank.

"Heaven only knows," replied Albie. "He's a strange one. Everyone says he's an egomaniac, but I have a different idea entirely."

"Oh?"

"Yes," said Albie. "Low self-esteem. That's how I read it. Anyway, I have to go. I have stacks of work to get through."

"Are you coming in this weekend?" asked Frank. "Remember, you said you'd help me with my rollerblades. And there's going to be a concert in Golden Gate Park. I could pack a lunch."

"Good idea!" said Albie. He loved San Francisco, the weather was supposed to be good and he relished the idea of spending the day in the city, and maybe going dancing at night. "I'll come by your place around ten on Saturday."

"Be good, now," said Frank.

"Hugs," said Albie automatically.

Putting down the phone Albie became uncomfortably aware that a man was standing at the counter of his station. Albie didn't know how long this fellow had been waiting, and how much he had heard. But he obviously wasn't a customer, so the situation couldn't be too serious, even if he had overheard everything.

"Yes?" said Albie tentatively.

Fenelon said "I'm here from Building Fifteen? Arthur Smith."

"I see that from your badge," smiled Albie. This guy was cute! "How may I help you?"

"I'm supposed to be getting acquainted with some of the other departments," said Fenelon. "Didn't Toni Hunter call you?"

"Probably she did," said Albie, "but to tell you the truth I'm a little behind on my voicemail. Maybe you could refresh my mind as to who you're going to see?"

"Well," said Fenelon pulling out a piece of paper from his jacket pocket and consulting it, "there's quite a list here. Seven, no, eight people, starting with Mr. Salamon."

"Let me see that, please," said Albie, taking the paper from Fenelon. "Most of these people are here today. I can probably get you in. I'm really sorry I didn't have this all set up for you. I'm generally better organized than this. Let's see. You'd better start with King, because he's very hard to find. Usually he's out traveling around the world, but this week he's here defending his turf."

"Oh," smiled Fenelon. "He must be the person you were talking about. The one they're trying to get to move? I'm sorry, I couldn't help overhearing you talking to your girlfriend."

"My possible boyfriend, actually," said Albie. "Let me see if I can get you in." He picked up the phone and started to dial a number.

"Wait a minute," said Fenelon. "Do you know someone named Rob MacDougal who used to work here?"

"Robbie, sure! I know him. A really good guy. But he's still here!"

"No, he's not," said Fenelon. "He's just started to work in our division. I got introduced to him this morning."

Albie said "Well, now that he's no longer here, it can be told. He got shafted by King. He should be running a PR group, you know. I gotta say, sometimes I wonder about the way things are run around here."

"I heard his story," said Fenelon. "He seems to have been treated really badly."

"That's my buddy King," said Albie with a shrug. "Anyway, he might not be here too much longer, from what I hear. I think he's going up a rung or two. He's always treated me OK, I don't know why. But his direct reports—he can be pretty vicious to them."

"Well, Rob told me to watch out for him. Put on my kid gloves, and all that. What do you think?"

"You don't have to worry," said Albie, reaching again for the phone. "You're in software, and King's in hardware. Never the twain shall meet. I'm kind of surprised you guys found a place for Rob in your operation."

"We use PR, too," said Fenelon.

WHEN FENELON AND King had finished with the social niceties King began expounding on hardware, and especially how the company had been going down the wrong track chipwise and vendorwise, and every other wise, and how he thought things could be vastly improved. He found ways of dropping the names of the highest company executives into every sentence, it seemed. Fenelon noticed, however, that King seemed to be treating him with wary respect, even with deference. His fame as a software genius seemed to have seeped into the hardware division.

While King was talking, Fenelon had the chance to sneak occasional glimpses of the office they were in. It was a very nice one, with lots of windows, and the view of the pond that Albie had described to Frank on the phone. Fenelon recalled that in Building Fifteen Rob MacDougal had been stuck in a converted storage space which had been outfitted with a phone and a desk. The Facilities people were still trying to decide how to connect MacDougal's system to the net.

Finally King ran out of steam and settled back, looking at Fenelon expectantly. "I know, never mind how, that you're involved with Nemo. What I'm trying to say is, we've gotta align our forces in this company—hardware, software, everyone's gotta get behind the direction. I know that Nemo is going to lead the way over the next few years. When you guys go public, I mean internally, I hope you and I can work closely together."

"I'm looking forward to it," said Fenelon. "I know that Kyle is big on this interdivisional cooperation."

"He is, yeah." said King, fiddling with a pencil on his desk. "Kyle's got the right stuff, all right."

"The thing I like about him," said Fenelon, "I hear he's not into status games. You know, like who's got the biggest car, or biggest office. I mean, look at his own office. He doesn't have anything like this," and Fenelon indicated the view over the pond. "Kyle really believes that the most important thing is being a team player.... Bury the ego, that sort of thing. From what I hear, of course.... I'm still new here."

King felt the tiniest nerve impulse flit across a synapse, somewhere deep within his brain. His ability to recognize such signals, and his willingness to act without hesitation on them, had contributed to his having attained those perfect scores on the Graduate Record exams, so many years ago. They had also served him well in the political aspects of his career at DataDrive.

"No, no," said King. "I see what you mean. You're right." King was acutely aware that his promotion to VP of hardware would be coming up at Kyle's staff within two or three weeks. He had been told, of course, that this was *pro forma* only. Still....

"You know," said King, "I've gotta enjoy the view here as much as I can today. Tomorrow I'm moving down the hall. We've got a little space problem in the building." There! That ought to set the record straight with this miserable creep! Anyway, soon he'd be in an office that would make this one look like a stable.

"Wow!" said Fenelon. "It must be hard to contemplate moving from a nice place like this."

"No sacrifice too great," smiled King. "So who're you going to see next?"

# fourteen

FELICIA SHADROE HAD a cleaning woman who came once a week for four hours to do the condo. The name of this woman was Dolorosa Contreras, and she came from a suburb of Hermosillo, in Mexico. The saga of how Dolorosa had risen from poverty in Mexico to being a cleaning lady in Aspen, Colorado, was not one involving as much social mobility as Dolorosa had hoped when she began her journey north. Yet she was quite content. She had seven families at present, and certainly Felicia gave her less trouble than anyone.

For one thing, Felicia did not make any to-do about social security and withholding taxes, the way some of her ladies did. Following the publicity surrounding certain female candidates for cabinet posts in Washington, whose hopes of attaining the levers of power had been dashed simply because they had failed to report the meager earnings of their housecleaners and babysitters to the Department of the Treasury, some of Dolorosa's Aspen clients had tried to get her to agree to do things "the legal way," as one of them had put it. Dolorosa was not interested in doing things the legal way. If she had been concerned with doing things the legal way she would be stuck in Hermosillo. She earned little enough as it was, and a substantial portion of her earnings found its way back to Mexico, where the effect was to keep several other family members from attempting the wearisome journey north themselves.

Eventually her ladies had given up. But Felicia, bless her, had never even considered getting involved with legal stuff. Dolorosa wasn't sure what Felicia did for a living. All she knew was that her client was always rushing off to airports. There was a son, Arthur, who lived in California and whom Dolorosa had never seen, but to whom Felicia wrote regularly. Dolorosa had often taken Felicia's letters to Arthur with her and mailed them at the Aspen post office.

When Dolorosa let herself into the condo on the afternoon of the day Arthur had left for California she found it in its usual spotless condition. She mopped and vacuumed and dusted nonetheless. When she got to Felicia's office she wiped off the desk, and saw the air ticket that Arthur had put on the chair. Examining it, Dolorosa saw Arthur's name. She instantly realized what had happened. Felicia had purchased this ticket for her son, so that the two could spend a few days together. But Felicia had gone off, probably on a trip, and had forgotten to send the ticket to Arthur. Dolorosa was not familiar with air transport. She had never been on an airplane. Nor did she have a firm command of English. So she didn't look closely at the fine print on the ticket. Otherwise she might have seen that the date of travel was that very day, and that it was a one way ticket *from* Aspen.

When Dolorosa left the condo she carried the ticket with her in an envelope that she herself had addressed to Arthur's apartment in Sunnyvale. She was quite proud of her printing.

In her search for a stamp, she had almost forgotten to pick up the sixty dollars in cash that Felicia had left for her under the sugar bowl in the kitchen. Forgetting the money—now that would have been a first for her!

## fifteen

"COME ON, BUDDY. How did you get your hands on those photos?" Fenelon and Chatterjee were in the Chevy on their way to Fremont for a real Indian home-cooked dinner. It was Thursday, the day after Fenelon and Sammi had had their lunch by the Bay.

"It wasn't difficult," Chatterjee said with a laugh. "The lucky part was in catching sight of the receptionist on her knees in front of your door, trying to get a clear shot. The mail slot was wide enough, but it was so close to the floor that she had to balance herself with one hand. I just walked up quietly behind her and waited. She must have used up a roll of film in two or three minutes."

"She probably didn't want to hang around long enough to get caught," said Fenelon.

"Judging from her reaction when she backed into me, I would say that you were right." And Chatterjee laughed some more. "I had not heard such squawks of sheer terror since the time a large snake got into my grandfather's chicken yard. I am amazed that you were not aware of them."

"You have never been, shall we say, fully engaged with Ms. Hunter," Fenelon said a bit moodily.

"True enough," said Chatterjee. "Anyway, since it is strictly forbidden for anyone to enter the labs who is not entitled to be there," and at this he shot Fenelon a meaningful look, "and since, furthermore, it is strictly forbidden for *anyone* to take a camera into the labs, I had Carmelita on two counts, as we might say. It was an easy task to persuade her to give up her camera on a temporary basis, and to get her to surrender the rolls of film she had taken on previous days. Fortunately, she had not been able to work out how and where to develop them. They were all reposing in her purse."

"Which raises the question of how you got them developed," said Fenelon. "And by the way, why didn't you just turn them over to me? After all, they are rather intimate."

"You may as well ask why I didn't turn them over to Toni Hunter, my friend. "The shots are just as intimate so far as she is concerned. Perhaps more so, especially the one where she appears to be..."

"Never mind," said Fenelon. "But tell me, how on earth did you get those things printed? I mean, you didn't just take them to the supermarket, did you?"

"No need," said Chatterjee. "My cousin in Oakland runs a photo shop and knows all about how to develop and print photos. He resisted turning the negatives back over to me. He seemed to think that several could be quite marketable in India. But since I have some money invested in his business I was able to prevail. That is how you come to have the negatives now."

"My God!" said Fenelon. "I might have been on display in every bazaar in India!"

"You and Toni, yes. Of course, not openly. One would have had to inquire of the shopkeeper." And Chatterjee roared with laughter.

"To tell you the truth, I'm glad it's over," Fenelon said. "Toni isn't my type. She always made me think her mind was somewhere else."

"It was not her mind that mattered at those moments, I am sure," said Chatterjee. "In any case, I am not sure it is over. After she recovered from her surprise, and had agreed to help us find Arthur Smith, she seemed to become quite good humored. Almost natural, in fact. She said to me, 'I knew he couldn't be a software genius. He looks much more like a poet.' I believe she is quite taken with you, perhaps more than ever now that she knows you are, well, normal."

"Well I'll be damned," said Fenelon.

"Turn off the highway at the next exit, please. Now you take this boulevard for two miles."

"How many people are coming to dinner?"

"Eight," said Chatterjee, "counting us. My sister, of course. Two engineers from other companies, and their spouses. My auntie from Calcutta makes eight. Of course, there will be some children there as well, but they will eat at a separate table. My sister and auntie have been preparing the food all day. My sister took the day off from work for the occasion."

"You promised me that there would be no brains this time," said Fenelon.

"I promise you, the only brains there will be those belonging to the diners. Though you seemed to enjoy the dish when you had it at the Silk Saree. As I recall, you had the lion's share."

"Remember, I'm from Indiana. I have a delicate stomach."

"No, my friend. You are a Californian now. You can no longer use Indiana as an excuse for anything. Besides, I would like to inform you that Indiana is not as benighted as you would have me believe. I have been there and it is a most beautiful state. With excellent educational institutions, may I add."

"That's a sore point with me," said Fenelon.

"Yes, I understand. But I would also like you to consider this: your failure to achieve tenure may, in fact, have been related to your unwillingness to play the politics of the situation. I recall your telling me a story about the parking lot at your college. You might have arranged a bit more status for yourself had you waited a while and become closer to those who actually disposed of the parking places."

Fenelon was shocked. "Wait just a minute! You've been telling me since I met you about how all this political bull does is waste time and energy. And now you tell me I should've played their game all along?"

"Moderation is the key," said Chatterjee calmly. "You do not want to become a Jerzy Bobochek. On the other hand, you do not want to let people walk all over you."

Fenelon could think of nothing to say.

"Turn left at the next street," said Chatterjee. "We are almost there. This is my house, the one with the cars in front."

Fenelon parked the car and turned to Chatterjee. "One thing," he said.

"Yes?"

"I'm not whining, understand? I'm not complaining. But I didn't have a great-grandfather who was a famous Bengali poet, and I didn't go to any selective schools. If I had got my doctorate from Harvard or Yale, things..." But he had to stop. Chatterjee's hands were waving about in the air over his head.

"Fenelon, I will only say this once, because it embarrasses me to have to contradict you and destroy the protective wall you seem determined to maintain at all costs, namely a wall of failure. You have a doctorate, and in the humanities. Do you realize what a great thing this is? You are not only an educated man, you are a scholar, and from what I have deduced you are, or were, a great teacher. Yes! Do not say anything! You told me that your classes were extremely popular, and not only with the young women! You told me that your class on Villon and Marot had a waiting list. A waiting list! How many professors of early French literature have students fighting to get into their classes?

"You have a very good mind. True, it is not a technological mind, but so what? You are resourceful and handsome and clever and popular, and you can be deceptive when necessary. This is wonderful! And you wanted to be a waiter? Hah!" Chatterjee delivered himself of these last words with considerable force. Then he opened the door and swiveled out of the car. Fenelon got out too, and walked with his friend to the door of the small one-story house. For some reason he was starting to feel pretty good about things.

FOUR HOURS LATER all the guests had left, sleepy children in tow. Chatterjee's auntie, whose name Fenelon had been unable to grasp, had plunked herself down next to him on the sofa. Sandhya, Chatterjee's sister, was in the kitchen, having refused all Fenelon's pleas to be allowed to help. "Men not allowed in the kitchen!" she said.

"But I want to help," Fenelon had said. He was also eager to engage Sandhya in conversation. There had been so many people, it seemed, and the conversation had been so fast and furious that he had not really had a chance to get to know her. After all, she was the hostess. But she had been insistent that he "go relax," as she had put it, and indeed Fenelon felt that some relaxation after the experience of his first home-cooked Indian feast was probably indicated. Chatterjee was off somewhere in another room, probably his little office, which he had shown to Fenelon with pride. The office boasted two large bookcases, an easy chair, and a desk with a huge computer monitor on it. The computer itself hummed on the floor next to the desk.

Chatterjee's auntie said "So, you are long with the DataDrive company?"

"It seems like quite a while," said Fenelon. "But in fact I've only been there a few weeks."

"My nephew tells me you are very clever," said Chatterjee's auntie. "You are not married?" Fenelon had stopped wearing his wedding band while working at the diner in Winnemucca, Nevada.

"I don't think so," said Fenelon. "I think by now I am divorced."

"Oh, I see," she said. "Divorced. You have children, perhaps?"

"Yes, two. A boy and a girl. It seems like another life, though. I don't have the kids. My wife has them, and since I'm here and they are in Indiana I guess I won't be having much contact for a while, except by phone."

"Oh. Ranjan told me you do not like to use the phone."

"That's true, while I'm working. But I have called the kids a couple of times from my apartment."

"You have a very good job, my nephew tells me. He also tells me that you are a very kind person."

Fenelon smiled. "I don't think I'm especially kind."

"He tells me that you get along very well with everyone at the company. It is so hard to get along with the engineers, I always think. They are so narrow, really. It seems all they can think about is their work. And Ranjan tells me that you even have good relations with the people in the Human Resources department. Poor things! No one really seems to like them at all, from what I hear."

"Oh, they're all right," said Fenelon, a trifle uneasily.

At this moment Chatterjee appeared at the opening that led to the hall. "Auntie," he called. "Could you come here for just a minute, please. I need to show you the papers for Haresh Nanda's estate."

"Haresh is my uncle on my father's side," said Chatterjee's auntie, rising. "He passed away several weeks ago, and I am the executrix of his estate. It is all very complicated. Thank goodness I have good lawyers at home, and my nephew here to assist me." Chatterjee guided her from the room, turning and looking back at Fenelon.

"Why don't you go chat with Sandhya in the kitchen?" he said. "She is making tea, and I believe we are going to have some sweets."

"More food?" groaned Fenelon, but he got up and went toward the kitchen. Sandhya stuck her head around the corner of the opening between the kitchen and dining area and smiled at him.

"I've been sent here by your brother," Fenelon said.

"Come, you are welcome."

Sandhya was fairly tall, and wore a beautiful green sari. Because Chatterjee was Fenelon's best friend in California, and certainly ranked equally with Emile on a worldwide friendship scale, ever since entering the house, Fenelon had done his best to avoid thinking of Sandhya in a sexual way. But this was very difficult, since she was rather lovely. Her eyes were astoundingly dark and deep, and her complexion was smooth and clear. Fenelon guessed her to be perhaps twenty-eight or -nine. He knew that she was younger than Chatterjee, but he had never asked his friend's age. He had just estimated him to be in the low thirties. He knew that Sandhya kept house for Chatterjee and that she worked in an office of some kind, but other than that she was a complete mystery. Fenelon had always been under the impression that Indian girls were married off by the age of thirteen, so he could not imagine why this beautiful creature didn't have a husband and at least four or five children as well.

He perched on a small stepladder and watched her move about the tiny kitchen. Suddenly she turned to him and said, "Have you nothing to say?"

"What do you do?" Fenelon blurted out. Sandhya smiled and put her hands on her small waist.

"How infernally American that is! Practically the first words you've spoken to me all evening, and you want to know 'what I do!' Well, it is a start, at any rate. I am an accountant. A CPA, to be exact. I work mostly with smaller businesses and some individuals. Do you need an accountant?"

Fenelon realized with a start that come tax time he might well need more than an accountant. He might also need a ticket to some place farther away than Death Valley. To a country, if there was one, that didn't have an extradition treaty with the United States. Famous gangsters, such as Al Capone, had been brought low not by the laws against bootlegging, extortion or murder, but by the tax laws. He wasn't sure how he would be able to handle both his own tax return and Arthur Smith's as well. He knew that at the bottom of Form 1040 there was a little line that said "Sign here if prepared by someone other than taxpayer," or some words to that effect. Should he sign "Arthur Smith" on the taxpayer line, and his own name on the "prepared by somebody else" line? And should he combine his income as a professor of French language and literature with Arthur's income? The diner in Winnemucca had paid him under the table in cash, and he certainly wasn't going to declare the tips he had collected, so he wasn't worried about that.

"Fenelon, what in the world is the matter with you?" asked Sandhya, coming over to him. She put her hand on his forehead. He realized that he was sweating. Her hand felt very cool, and she was standing right in front of him. Her breasts rose and fell with solicitude under the green *choli*. "You are obviously not used to spicy food. Like all good things, it takes some time to get used to."

"No, it's not that," he muttered. "I'm just worried about something."

Sandhya removed her hand, went to the sink, and returned with a damp cloth with which she wiped his forehead. "Go and sit down again in the living room. Put your head back. I will bring the tea in a minute."

Fenelon did as he was told.

# sixteen

HE DAY AFTER Toni had vowed her wholehearted cooperation in the search for the real Arthur Smith, Fenelon was in possession of Arthur's personnel file. He learned some interesting things about Arthur, among which was the date of his birth. Arthur was thirty years old, and would turn thirty-one three weeks from now. If he was still alive, of course. Fenelon found himself wondering whether perhaps Judd Trainor, the recruiter who had provided virtually all of the personal information on Arthur that was in the file, had had an ulterior motive. Why else should a recruiter have bothered to get all this information? For instance, Arthur's insurance beneficiary was his mother, Felicia Shadroe. Why was there a difference in the last names? Had Arthur assumed the pseudonym of Smith because he wanted to avoid his mother? But if so, why would he have made his mother the beneficiary of his life insurance?

In one of those moments of lucidity that sometimes illuminate the knottiest of problems, Fenelon suddenly saw the answer. Who was to say that Felicia was Arthur's mother at all? Arthur doubtless had had a fat company-paid life insurance policy while at his former employer. Judd and a woman named Felicia could have formed a plot. If Arthur had died while still on the payroll at Siegfried Software he could have done something odd, such as leaving all his insurance money to benefit indigent software developers. There were certainly enough of them out on the street these days. But if Arthur could be lured to another company—Data-Drive, for example—he would then have a *new* insurance policy. The poor simple devil could have been conned into appointing the Queen of Sheba as sole beneficiary. And that was exactly what Judd Trainor and Felicia had brought about, except that Felicia was the beneficiary, of course, not the Queen of Sheba.

Come to think of it, Fenelon now recalled that the insurance documents he had signed upon joining Datadrive had *already* borne the name of Felicia Shadroe! At the time, he had been too nervous to question this.

One could test the plot theory by getting a look at Arthur's insurance application in his file at Siegfried Software, of course. The police ought to be able to do that easily enough. Except, of course, he *couldn't* go to the police, nor could Chatterjee, because that would mean he, Fenelon, would be exposed as an imposter.

The plot couldn't have worked, he realized, unless Toni had been in on it as well. Obviously someone in HR had to be aware that all the personal information in Arthur's file had come from a recruiter, and not directly from Arthur. And this would have been highly unusual. So there *had* to be an accomplice in HR.

And then the light dawned on poor Fenelon, whose brain was beginning to whirl out of control. The inside accomplice was Daphne, of course. The innocent-seeming, mousy HR admin. Of course, she was just a pawn. Judd had no doubt charmed her. Sex was probably the lever that opened Daphne's innocence to corruption. And behind Judd there loomed... Felicia. The woman he was about to telephone.

The phone rang four or five times in the Aspen condo, and

Fenelon was about to put the receiver down with relief, when he heard a click on the line and a woman's voice said "Felicia Shadroe speaking."

For some reason, Fenelon had been expecting a younger voice, perhaps one with some sex appeal. This voice seemed somehow... well traveled, and as though it had picked up some gravel on the way. Fenelon cleared his throat. "Excuse me, Ms. Shadroe," he began, but could go no farther because the voice interrupted him sharply.

"That's Mrs. Shadroe. Not Ms."

"I'm sorry," Fenelon began again.

"That's perfectly all right. It's just that I believe strongly in family values, and as you may know from my writings, I hold that using the contrived title 'Ms.' is but one of a number of seemingly minor, but nonetheless noxious linguistic assaults on those values."

"Linguistic assaults?" said Fenelon.

"I assume I am speaking to the *Times*," said the voice.

"Well, your assumption is wrong," said Fenelon. He was getting upset. "I'm not the *Times*."

"Then for heaven's sakes get off the line! I am expecting a call just at this moment from the reviewer at the *Times*. He has my latest book and wants to... oh, what's the use! State your business quickly and then hang up, or I will."

"This is the Human Resources department at Datadrive, in Mountain View, California," said Fenelon evenly. "We are trying to locate your son, Arthur Smith."

There was a pause on the line. Then the voice said "Arthur? But he is there! He should have been there days ago. He was to discuss the terms of his employment with you people. I think it is disgraceful for you to get him to agree to join you, without your ever even mentioning the question of salary!"

"Yes," said Fenelon. "But that doesn't help us to locate your son. You see, he hasn't shown up here at all."

"Hasn't shown up? Why, I gave him an air ticket and he flew to San Jose with it!"

"You gave him an air ticket from Sunnyvale to San Jose?" said Fenelon.

The voice said, "You are being facetious! Don't you dare! I have influence at Datadrive, I'll have you know!"

"Mrs. Shadroe," said Fenelon, "we only want to know where Arthur is. We're concerned about him. We need his brain."

"The only thing I can think of is that he must be at home with a cold. Ever since he was a little boy he would forget to get warmly dressed when he went outdoors. He was delicate, too, and really shouldn't have gone outside at all. But of course a mother can't refuse her little boy's entreaties."

"Does he have a girl friend?" asked Fenelon in desperation.

"Certainly not! If he had I would have known about it. Arthur hides nothing from his mother."

"Well, thanks anyway," said Fenelon.

"Wait a minute! I didn't get your name!" said Felicia.

"It's not important," said Fenelon.

"My boy's being missing is very important," said Felicia. "I am calling a senior official right now."

"Goodbye," said Fenelon, and as he put the phone down he turned to see Chatterjee standing in his office door. "God! I thought the mother might have plotted to murder the son. Now I see I had it all backwards. If anyone was motivated to kill his mother it had to be Arthur." And he told Chatterjee about the conversation he had just had.

"Felicia Shadroe?" said Chatterjee. "I know who she is! She is a columnist for a bunch of right-wing papers. Sometimes she appears on television shows. She has climbed firmly onto the barricades defending this country against being taken over by the queers and abortionists. I believe she is also not friendly to immigrants of color, though the other kind appears to be acceptable."

"Wait a minute!" said Fenelon excitedly. "What if Arthur is gay? Maybe that's why he changed his name! His mother may have paid him to do it, so that she could keep writing against homosexuals."

Chatterjee waved his arms over his head. "My friend, calm yourself. Remember, we are only trying to find Arthur, not delve deeply into his family relationships. Besides, from what I know of Felicia Shadroe, she is quite capable of fulminating against gays on the one hand, while making an exception for her own son on the other. You must remember that such people are not concerned that their actions appear logical. They are motivated by money, or by fear or hatred, caused by some horrible thing that happened to them when they were little."

"Nurture rather than nature, then?" said Fenelon.

"Exactly. For example, Felicia herself could have been brought up by honest, godfearing parents. The worst thing that can happen to an impressionable child."

Fenelon was prevented from exploring this fascinating statement by the sound of loud footsteps in the hall. Chatterjee moved swiftly across the outer office and disappeared a moment before Jerzy Bobochek's large frame bulked into view.

"Ah, there you are!" he said. "I knew she was mistaken. 'He's been here all along,' I told her. But of course she wouldn't believe me. So I thought I'd check for myself. How are things, Arthur? By the way, I'm Jerzy."

"Yes, I've seen you around," said Fenelon, shaking Jerzy's hand.

"Your mother called me just a minute ago with some crazy story about a call from some guy in our HR department saying you weren't here. Of course I knew there was something wrong right away, because we don't have any guys in our HR department. They're all women, of course. Except for the VP. He's a man, of course, even if he's a bit of an empty suit. Well, I got to be going.

Don't worry about your mother. I'll call her and give her the good news. We used to know each other slightly; that's why she called me, I guess."

"OK," said Fenelon.

"By the way," said Jerzy, turning in the doorway. "You don't look like your typical software man. You look more on the rangy side. The guys around here sit on their asses too much, eat too much junk food. They told me that we had to install those machines in there to keep you happy. The turkeys! Shows you what HR knows. Eating junk food! Interested in politics?"

This last question came so quickly that Fenelon confused it with the remark about junk food. "A bit," he said.

"Good! I belong to an organization that you might be interested in joining. I'd tell you about it but I gotta run. How about doing lunch next week?"

"Fine," said Fenelon.

"Great. By the way, I wouldn't mind having just one bag of those Kachina chips. I'll just grab it if you don't mind. They're out of them in the break room."

"I'll get it," Fenelon said hastily, and he quickly went into the adjoining room to do so.

WHEN JERZY HAD moved safely down the hall Fenelon went back into the next room and looked down at Chatterjee, who was perched on the rolled-up futon, laughing silently. "What are you snickering about?" he said sourly. "If he had come in here after those chips your goose would have been cooked."

Chatterjee wiped his eyes. "Life around you is certainly eventful," he said. "I assume the coast is clear now? Or is Ms. Hunter about to come in for a, shall we say, refill?" And he guffawed.

Fenelon sat down beside him. "I don't want to hear anything about Toni, or Jerzy. I wish I were out of this place. And by the way, why did you cut and run just now?"

Chatterjee tried to compose his face. "It would not help my

career to be found associating too closely with someone who may soon be in durance vile."

"You mean, in prison?" said Fenelon with horror.

"All will be well, my friend, as soon as we find Arthur."

"But we can't! He's either been murdered, or he's just vanished. We'll never find him."

"We are not thinking clearly enough, that is all. What do we know about him? That he has a mother in Aspen, Colorado. That he is a software genius. That he likes a certain brand of corn chips. That his tastes are simple."

"And," added Fenelon, "along that line, that he doesn't like the telephone. And that he doesn't drive."

"He doesn't?" said Chatterjee. "But you *do* drive."

"Very funny," said Fenelon.

"No, I mean people, people here, have seen you drive, and no one has remarked on it as exceptional. It is quite normal these days to drive a car. So how do you, who have never met this Arthur Smith, know that he does not drive? For all you know he might be a champion on the Le Mans circuit."

"I know," said Fenelon slowly, "because someone told me."

"Who?"

"I can't remember. It was early during my stay here."

"But no one knew this fact! Surely it cannot have been in his personnel file."

"That's it!" cried Fenelon. "I found out from that girl, the admin, who processed me into this madhouse. She has a classical name...."

"Daphne," said Chatterjee.

"Daphne," said Fenelon.

"Now we are getting somewhere," said Chatterjee. "You said Mrs. Shadroe told you she had bought a ticket for her son Arthur to fly to San Jose to go to work. Or to negotiate something...."

"Salary," said Fenelon.

"Where was this voyage to begin? Obviously, in Aspen. There is an airport there, I suspect, or nearby, what with all the wealthy people who sojourn there. But since the trip began in Aspen the question is naturally, how did Arthur get to Aspen?"

"A friend drove him, or he flew."

"No, no!" said Chatterjee, and his hands went up over his head. "You are clearly not a software genius. Being driven by a friend would have required actually soliciting such a favor, which would have been a normal social interaction, and therefore very difficult for a true software genius such as Arthur to have done. Besides, why didn't the friend drive him back to California? Did he deposit Arthur at his mother's, and then drive back alone?

"As for flying there, first, Arthur would have had to disturb the normal flow of his life to have the thought of taking a plane, and second, he would have had to go to an airline office, since he didn't use the telephone, and purchase a ticket."

"So why didn't he do that? He had the money!"

"My friend," said Chatterjee gently, "I doubt very much that Arthur Smith is even aware that money exists for any purpose other than fast computers, fast food, and the occasional pizza. You must never forget, he is a genius! In any case, he would have bought a round-trip ticket, so there would have been no need for his mother to buy another. But we know she did!"

"So what *did* he do?"

Chatterjee rose from the futon. "It is very very evident to me now. What happened was that Arthur took the easy way out. He rode his bicycle to Aspen, beginning on the day he was recruited, or shortly thereafter."

Fenelon stared at him. "My God, Chatterjee—it's affecting you, too! You've gone nuts! The easy way out? To ride your bike, what is it, a thousand miles or more? Up and down the Rockies? To visit your mother? When you should be at work?" He put his hands to his head.

Chatterjee was unaffected. "He spent some days with his mother, and then he set out again for California. And that is where he is right now."

"*Where?*" cried Fenelon.

"On a road between there and here. If we wait long enough he will show up. Unfortunately, every day counts. I need him now. Fortunately his choice of routes is limited. All we need to know is when exactly he left Aspen, and we can calculate approximately where he should be now. I would suggest we use the same rate of travel as that of his trip to Aspen from here, but increasing his daily distance by perhaps ten percent."

Fenelon had given up a few moments earlier, but this last remark of Chatterjee's stirred his curiosity. "Why ten percent faster on the return trip?" he asked. "Is it the effect of the wind?"

"Of course not," said Chatterjee. "What wind there is will probably come from the west. No, it is just that Arthur will obviously be in better physical condition coming back, because of the training effect of the ride out."

"Of course," said Fenelon.

"May I use your phone?" said Chatterjee? Fenelon slowly got to his feet and they went into the outer office.

"Now, is this Felicia Shadroe's number? Ah, yes, I see it is." And Chatterjee dialed it. Then he said "Hello? Is this Mrs. Shadroe? Yes, this is the *Times* calling. No, Mrs. Shadroe, the *Times* of London, not the *Times* of New York. Of course we have. Your views are widely read here and, might I add, are shared by a number of us on the editorial staff. No, no, not at all. Now dear Mrs. Shadroe, we have heard that your son is missing. Yes, Arthur Smith. We have no intention of intruding upon your personal feelings, of course, but because we are admirers, we.... Yes, quite. Yes, they certainly are. Officials of large corporations often become confused, in our opinion. Now Mrs. Shadroe, when did you last see your son? Oh. And when did he arrive in Aspen? Yes, I see. On his bicycle, did he?" and at this point Chatterjee grinned up at Fenelon, who was standing by his side.

"Is his bicycle still at your home, Mrs. Shadroe? Ah, it isn't. Yes, perhaps it was stolen. Yes, even in such a nice place as Aspen. It is truly a shame…. By the way, did it have a light on it? I see. Well, we must all do our bit, mustn't we? Keep up the writing, Mrs. Shadroe. I understand it is appreciated even in the Royal Household. But please don't tell that to anyone. I know I can trust you. Yes, well, goodbye for now." And Chatterjee put down the phone.

Fenelon looked at him in admiration.

"We will start in twenty-four hours," said Chatterjee excitedly. "I will make all the arrangements and I will calculate where he should be, within one or two hundred miles. We will find him, and quickly. Never fear!"

"Wait," said Fenelon. I have two questions. First, how the hell are we going to find Arthur? I mean, get a message to him? He's on a bike, for God's sake!"

"That is easy. We will fly over the roads and we will see him on his bike. We will land on the road, or nearby, and we will speak with him."

Fenelon gaped at him. "Fly? You mean, a plane? Where are we going to… this is crazy! A plane! You mean a little one?"

"One cannot fly in a Boeing at the low altitude required to spot Arthur Smith," said Chatterjee, a bit primly. "From the heights required for a commercial airplane, Arthur Smith would not be visible. As for landing…."

"I know," said Fenelon heavily. "But there are just a few practical problems, like where are we going to get a plane? And a pilot crazy enough to do what you're thinking?"

"Again, easy. My sister has a male friend who belongs to a flying club. He has access to a plane. A very nice one, too, if a bit old. A Cessna 172. My sister will get her friend to fly us along the roads. Though I must take exception to your characterizing her friend as 'crazy.' The government does not license the insane to fly aircraft."

"You mean, Sandhya has a boyfriend?"

"A boy he is not," said Chatterjee. "Now your second question?"

"No matter," said Fenelon.

"I see," said Chatterjee.

"Chatterjee," said Fenelon, " I was thinking of perhaps asking Sandhya to go out sometime. But if there's a boyfriend... well, I guess what I'm asking is, do you think she likes me enough to...."

"My dear friend, you certainly do not entertain any serious ideas with respect to my sister, I hope. You are not Indian, and in particular you are not Bengali. You are also not a Brahmin, and you eat meat," said Chatterjee severely.

"Wait a minute!" said Fenelon. "*You* eat meat! Remember the curried brains? And so does Sandhya! And your auntie...."

"I admit it," said Chatterjee, "though should you ever get to Calcutta please do not go spreading the news about. Now I have lost the thread. What was your question again? Yes, now I remember it. And the answer is, Yes, Fenelon. I can say that my sister does like you. I happen to know it for a fact. How Gopal fits into the picture I have no idea. Sandhya is an extremely strong-willed person, however. And now I must leave. If I am not very much mistaken, at any moment Jerzy will return to make sure he really did see you on his first visit. Felicia is a very persistent woman, and after that inquiry from the London *Times*...."

# seventeen

THE FOLLOWING DAY, at about two p.m., Fenelon was trying to read some documentation having to do with disk drives. He couldn't understand how so much information could fit into such a small space, even though he knew it was all due to electronics. He had just reached the conclusion that the technical paper in his hands was not going to answer this question, at least not in terms he could relate to, when there came a knock on the door of his office. He called out, and the door opened to admit a somewhat portly man dressed in a suit. There was a DataDrive badge clipped to the lapel of his jacket, and on the badge was a little gold medallion. That meant, Fenelon knew, that the wearer had been with the company for at least five years.

In the last few days Fenelon had noticed that there were plenty of portly people in the labs, but he had seen none of them wearing a suit. In fact, the joke around DataDrive was that unless you were in sales,  if you were wearing a suit you must be interviewing for a job.

"Arthur Smith?" asked the man.

Fenelon saw that this person was somewhat older than the norm for the labs. The norm appeared to be around twenty-five or so, and this man had to be in his late forties, at least. Absurdly, Fenelon felt a surge of gratitude. "What can I do for you?" he asked. "Have a seat."

"I'm also Arthur," said the man, "but I go by Art. Art Zilkowski. Ranjan Chatterjee suggested I come see you about a little problem I've got," said the man, sitting in one of Fenelon's guest chairs.

"Yes," said Fenelon. "I'm not sure what I can do about anyone's problem, but fire away. Do you know Chatterjee from the lab?"

"Oh no. In fact, I really don't know him at all. I got to him through his sister, who is my sister's accountant."

Fenelon felt a little confused, but realizing that this story in some way involved Sandhya Chatterjee, gave an encouraging nod.

"My sister has a small business, a gift shop in Albany."

"You mean, Albany, New York?" asked Fenelon.

"No. Albany, California. It's near Berkeley. Anyway, Mary, that's my sister, has this accountant. She was talking to her about my problem, and the accountant suggested that I call her brother, who also works for DataDrive."

"And what is your problem?" asked Fenelon, who was beginning to feel impatient.

"I work in hardware, in documentation management. There are about forty of us over in Building Twelve in Cupertino. At least, we were working there until about six weeks ago. They closed the operation then and moved it to Texas."

"To Texas?" said Fenelon. "Why to Texas? It'll cost the company a fortune to move forty people to Texas."

Zilkowski smiled thinly. "I don't think you get the picture," he said. "The company isn't moving anybody. Well, that's not true, actually. They're moving three people. Two are level 12, and one is a 13."

"So what happens to the rest?" asked Fenelon.

"Well, we had a choice. We could move ourselves to Texas. Or we could find another job. HR gave us two months to look around. I've got two weeks left."

Fenelon was stunned. "I see you've been here for some time," he said, indicating Zilkowski's badge.

"Seven years," said Zilkowski.

Fenelon mused for a bit. "You only had two months' notice?"

"To be honest, we did see it coming some time ago. There are leaks all over this company, of course, like everywhere in the Valley. Until it was official, of course, we couldn't really start looking very hard. And I confess, I guess I personally was sort of in denial. I didn't really start putting the word out that I was looking until just before it became official."

"And moving to Texas...?"

"Doesn't appeal to me," said Zilkowski. "First of all, my wife works at DataDrive, too. We're both grade 11, so she's pulling in some decent money. And she doesn't want to start looking for a job, especially not in Texas. I checked into how much it would cost to move us there. With all our stuff it would come to about forty thousand."

"What?" gasped Fenelon.

"Yes, it's expensive. Of course, paying that much assumes we could sell our house. I talked to a broker I know. She estimates we'd be down in equity about sixty, seventy thousand."

"Down?"

"Loss on the sale," said Zilkowski. "You know what's happened to real estate."

"I can't believe this company would simply dump someone, I mean lots of people, onto the street," said Fenelon.

"You must understand that moving work groups, or even whole divisions to Texas, or Florida, or wherever, so long as it's far away, is an old industry tactic," said Zilkowski. "The idea is you can clean out large numbers of people without lawsuits, just some unfavorable headlines for a while. The idea was introduced into high tech a few years ago. A really large mainframe company moved a whole division from Florida to Texas, and told everyone they were welcome to come along. At their own expense, of course. I think they borrowed the idea from the shoe industry, only of course, those people would have had to move to Brazil or Korea.

"But to answer your question, DataDrive doesn't dump people onto the street. There's a whole support structure in place to help us get jobs. In fact, most of my colleagues have already been placed. They got a jump on me and a couple of others, because they believed it would happen and got to work, instead of burying their heads in the sand."

"So what are you doing about it," asked Fenelon.

"Undergoing career counseling, revising my resume for each interview. Trying to build a network. Going to see lots of friends, all of whom are sympathetic. I've put in for several openings and got short-listed for a couple, but no results. And most of them are pending. You know, none of these managers ever make up their mind in a hurry. It seems to take about three months minimum, and they only give you two months. And by the time you find out about the openings there are usually some favored candidates lined up."

"How about other companies?"

Zilkowski smiled again. "I'm fifty-six years old, Arthur. In the Valley, that means you're ready for burial. And please don't tell me that age discrimination is illegal."

"That must be hard to take."

"Being ready for burial is awful," said Zilkowski with a laugh. "Especially since I'm still working on my bridge game."

They sat in silence for a while. Then Fenelon said, "What did Chatterjee have to say? He's kind of a miracle worker around here."

"What he said was, 'Go see Arthur Smith.' He says you're a mover and shaker. That you'll know what to do."

Fenelon groaned inwardly. He knew now that it had been a mistake to boast to Chatterjee about his encounter with King Salamon. "What exactly is your position now?" he asked, trying to think of an escape route, and finding none.

"I'm actually shortlisted for a job as a distribution development manager, in software. It's not in this division, of course, it's in Building Seven. I know there's one other internal candidate, who's this guy from the telesales organization. I hate to say it, but he's *got* a job, and telesales isn't going to go away any time soon. Then there are a couple of outsiders, I don't know who they are. The hiring manager is Bob Tremain. T-R-E-M-A-I-N."

"I'll see what I can do," said Fenelon, making a note and shifting around a bit in his chair to signal that the meeting was over.

Zilkowski rose and grasped his hand warmly. "Anything you can do," he said. "Anything at all, I'd really appreciate it."

As soon as his visitor had gone Fenelon reached for the phone and tried to call Chatterjee, but there was no reply. He had an uneasy feeling that Chatterjee was just letting the phone ring. He could, of course, have waited and eventually spoken to him personally. But a reckless and daring feeling was beginning to steal over him. Fenelon realized that his days as a DataDrive software guru were numbered, and though he wasn't sure exactly what the total number was, he felt rather certain that it was low. He reached for the phone again.

JERZY BOBOCHEK GLANCED at the little screen on his telephone and saw that it was Arthur Smith who was calling him. This was certainly unexpected, until he realized that he had never followed through on his rather vague invitation to have lunch. He knew the relationship Arthur had with Kyle and, from what he had heard, with Kyle's wife as well. He had wondered about this latter situation, which had reached a stage somewhere between murmur and rumor, but had decided that Kyle's wife would not allow herself to be compromised by anyone from the company, even a romantic-looking guy like Arthur Smith. Unless Kyle was into really kinky stuff, of course, and was making it a threesome. But Kyle came from Ohio, and although there might be plenty of deviant behavior in Los Altos Hills, Jerzy refused to admit the possibility of Kyle's participation.

"Arthur, how are ya?" said Jerzy warmly.

"I'm doing very well, thanks," came Fenelon's voice.

"You know, I've been meaning to call you about lunch," said Jerzy. "I've been swamped here."

"No problem," said Fenelon.

"We'll do it next week. Gimme a call around Tuesday."

"Sure," said Fenelon. "I wanted to talk with you just for a moment about a situation."

Jerzy said "Yeah?"

And Fenelon explained about his friend Art Zilkowski, and how helpful it would be if Jerzy could make a call on his behalf.

"Well, I don't know," said Jerzy. "I don't really think I can do that, because I don't know this man at all. I mean, how good is he? How do you know him? And if he's so good, how come he's out of a job?"

"Jerzy," said Fenelon, " this guy is really good. The best. He can do this job one hand tied behind his back. I heard about him when I was back at Siegfried Software. I was going to give Kyle a call about him, but then I thought, Jerzy really has the influence around here, even though this position's not in your division. But if you don't think it's appropriate...."

"Wait a second. What I could do is I could call the VP this guy Tremain works for. Hold on a minute," and Jerzy tapped on his keyboard and consulted an organization chart.

"Yeah, it's Anderson, Rolf Anderson. I know him real well. I'll give him a ring."

"When?" came Fenelon's voice.

"Jesus! What's going on here?" Jerzy thought, and replied evenly "Right now, Arthur. Don't worry about it. If you vouch for this guy that's all I need. I'll take care of it."

AND SO IT was that the very next day, at about four in the afternoon, a large package came from a well-known purveyor of spirits in Palo Alto. Inside was a jereboam of Veuve Cliquot Brut, and a note. The note said:

*Dear Arthur,*

*This morning I got a call from Bob Tremain. I got the job. I don't know how you did it, but I know it was you from my former admin, who got it from Tremain's admin, who got it from his boss's admin. Please accept this as a small token of gratitude.*

*I bought two of these, by the way. The second one you, I, my wife, my sister and Sandhya Chatterjee will drink at dinner at our house this Friday. Please come around six, and don't eat too much for the previous twenty-four hours. See address on enclosed card.*

*Art Zilkowski*

*P.S. Ranjan can't make it. He is going to be taking a couple of days off starting tomorrow on some special mission or other and he'll have piles of stuff to get done when he gets back, he says.*

Fenelon went into the next room and extracted a bag of Kachinas from the vending machine. Returning to his office he sat down and began to munch thoughtfully. For the first time in his life he began to think that top management might have rewards beyond the purely monetary. But after a little reflection he recovered his sanity.

'Mover and shaker,' indeed!

# eighteen

KYLE WINFIELD, PRESIDENT and CEO of DataDrive, was not a religious man, although while he was growing up his parents and he attended church on a regular basis. They did so because his dad was the leading member of the community, from the economic point of view, which was a point of view that really counted in central Ohio. And his mom was the leading member of society. So of course they went to church.

Kyle's dad had been the president of a very large manufacturer of heavy earth-moving equipment, in the days when America led the world in moving earth. As president, Kyle's father enjoyed very considerable financial rewards in terms of salary and bonuses. The bonuses were awarded from time to time by the board of directors, none of whose members had had any personal experience in moving earth, but all of whom could understand the numbers. Understanding the numbers was important.

If you know your earth-moving equipment history, you know that the day finally dawned when this mighty country could no longer claim pre-eminence in this field. The advantage had shifted to the Japanese and Koreans who were, in Kyle's dad's opinion, tricky bastards whom you couldn't trust. Of course, Kyle's dad had never visited Korea or Japan, although the company had sales offices in both places. In earlier years he was just too busy growing the business; and in later years the orders from these two countries dwindled to a trickle and finally disappeared altogether, except for a backhoe ordered for some mysterious purpose by the U.S. Embassy in Seoul.

The company's numbers kept going down and down. Fortunately for Kyle, who was attending expensive private schools, the compensation paid by the company to his father kept going up and up. The board of directors seemed to be aware of the superhuman effort being exerted by Kyle's father to save the business. Part of this effort consisted of lengthy visits to Washington, the outcome of which was a special tax on Japanese and Korean earth-moving equipment imported into this country. The tax was designed to give Kyle's dad's company a fighting chance to retain American jobs, as a certain Senator had expressed it in committee. The tax expired after five years, and it was a great shame that it didn't achieve everything that was expected of it. The Japanese and Korean manufacturers rationalized their operations even more, expanded into new markets in southern Asia and Europe, and even flew their best American customers to the Orient where they were treated like potentates, and provided with literally every conceivable inducement for making a favorable purchasing decision.

A few months before Kyle's dad's company closed its doors forever, the board of directors voted Kyle's dad a golden handshake in recognition for the many years he had put into the company. Kyle's dad was to continue for a year as a consultant, under a contract whose terms were really pretty terrific. And the golden handshake itself was a lump-sum payment of $2.3 million dollars.

Given this history it is no wonder that, if young Kyle had any religion at all left after surviving both Harvard College and Wharton, it was the worship of the marketplace. Though the marketplace had done little for the workers in the plant, or for the sales and marketing folks, it had been very kind to the Winfields. And if pushed to it, young Kyle would even have been able to defend what the free market had done to the workers at his father's former company. If they had been Koreans, for example, they would have abandoned their ceaseless efforts to unionize, and then they would have been able to enhance their productivity. 'Enhance' was one of young Kyle's favorite words. In that case the company might have avoided bankruptcy. Market theory clearly included workers. Even Marx knew that much. So the workers themselves being part of the market, they owed it to themselves and to their families and anyone else who depended on them for a roof over their heads and for sustenance, continually to review their situation and to improve their skills. Workers who let themselves get out of sync with the way the world was going only had themselves to blame. With state-of-the-art skills they could always move to where the jobs were more plentiful, or paid better. Thank God, in this country every man and woman had a car, so mobility was certainly not an issue.

Young Kyle had been spared the necessity of paying out on a mortgage every month, as his father had considerately bought his first house for him, so he had owned it free and clear. He had traded up well, so he had no mortgage on his present house, either. In fact, though this may seem strange, none of Kyle's neighbors' houses was burdened by debt, except for the one housing the compulsive gambler (there were also several secret alcoholics and drug addicts, as well as a cross-dresser, in various other homes). This was one of the reasons that Kyle's view of the operations of the marketplace, so far as these might have affected the citizenry, were unbiased by any exposure to financial pressure. At Harvard, young Kyle had once surreptitiously bought a left-wing publication, just to see what it was preaching. He had observed that all the radical opinions advanced therein came from people he had never heard of at all. This publication was printed on cheap paper, and the whole business reeked of  bias and anti-middle class prejudice of the worst kind.

Like most Americans, even some of those sleeping in the street in cartons, young Kyle classified himself and his parents as 'middle-class.' He knew that his family was reasonably well-off, but in prep school, young Kyle had fallen for a girl from a family with old money from New York. He had gone to a couple of parties at the Plaza at Christmastime. There he was made aware of the boundary between the middle-class and the truly rich. It made him feel both worse and better. Worse, because though the Winfields were first-class in central Ohio, they were sort of between business and economy class in New York. Better, because he knew that henceforth he could relate more easily to ordinary persons. They were all members of the same class.

So young Kyle grew up going through the motions of one of the innumerable sects of the Christian confession, and adhering like a limpet to the hull of the market religion. One of the devils of his religion was, of course, the unions. You didn't have to have a degree from Wharton to realize how the unions warped the marketplace, distorted prices, and generally fouled things up royally. That was why the unions had already lost most of their power in America. But, like Hercules wrestling with Antaeus, just when you got the union devil down on the ground and were rubbing his face in it, was when you had to be most careful that he didn't spring up stronger than before. Thank God, employees in the high tech industry wanted nothing to do with the unions. Stock-purchase and option plans, high salaries, and an ever expanding list of other benefits hadn't offered them so much as a handhold into Data-Drive. At least, not to date.

That was why young Kyle, only he wasn't known that way any-more, was concerned about the state of affairs in the software development division. More particularly, he was concerned about Jerzy Bobochek. Not that Kyle was concerned about Jerzy's layoffs per se. To remain competitive Kyle would have taken DataDrive through a series of layoffs, if necessary. Indeed, he was aware that layoffs, or in the current lingo, downsizing, were quite the rage these days. Many companies in quite good health were doing it, for fear of looking old-fashioned in an industry where being old-fashioned meant you were dead. It was like in the nineteenth century, Kyle often thought, when healthy people would purge themselves on general principle. Kyle, himself, had instructed his new corporate VP for HR to get rid of several hundred people, but of course this was done piecemeal, not with fanfare the way some of the largest companies were doing it, with headlines, brass bands and all. If you did it piecemeal you didn't have to take a reserve, and Kyle knew from his Wharton days that taking a reserve against the expenses of firing several hundred employees was something Data-Drive didn't need just at the moment.

No, Kyle could do the necessary, when it was necessary. But what he didn't like at all were the rumblings he'd been getting from the software division. He knew from Sammi Boyadjian that there had been some unpleasant things said at outplacement interviews about how the departing employees—most of whom appeared to be quite decent engineers—had been treated. He didn't bother to ask Sammi how he was privy to these comments. He knew Sammi had his ways. He also knew Jerzy was after Sammi's job. But even allowing for all this, he realized that he had a problem, and it seemed to be the personality and management style of Jerzy Bobochek.

A few weeks ago he had pulled Teeny Farlow aside after his regular Monday morning staff. Teeny, who despite his nickname, weighed at least three hundred pounds, was Kyle's most trusted lieutenant. He was nominally corporate VP for operations, but in fact he doubled for Kyle, sometimes functioning as Kyle's asshole. To be a top executive's asshole meant that you could be counted on to do anything that required swift, nasty action—anything that the top executive didn't want to be associated with personally, but that he wanted very much to happen. Not only was Teeny imposing in a physical sense, he also had a keen mind—one of the best Kyle had ever seen in operation. Kyle had known Teeny since college days, and had called him into DataDrive three years ago from UCLA, where Teeny had been teaching in the B school.

In Kyle's office they had each had coffee and a couple of crullers that Kyle's admin, Penelope, had brought in from a nearby bakery that affected a New York style.

"Teeny, we've got a problem in software," Kyle had said.

Teeny, who had his own sources, agreed. "Jerzy," he said.

"I think so. Could you look into it? He's making his numbers, but..."

"The guy's making his numbers. But he might drive the division out of business."

"Yeah," said Kyle. "And he's lost a lot of people. Some good ones."

"My wife told me maybe a year ago she got a call from some frantic woman, wife of one of those managers he fired right after he came on board. She was pretty upset, my wife, I mean. This was some friend of hers."

"I don't care so much about the managers," Kyle continued. "Nor about the engineers, for that matter. But he's doing it with no plan, no rationale other than to keep everyone off base. I understand he thinks that makes for a good working environment. Also he keeps knocking projects off the list at random. He's always got a story, of course."

Teeny snorted. "The guy's a dope."

"Well, look into it, would you? I don't like having a lot of discontent in the ranks. Lemme have a plan in a few days."

"Done," said Teeny, and hefted himself out of the chair and lumbered down the hall.

A COUPLE OF weeks later he met Kyle as arranged in a hamburg joint in Menlo Park, and did a core dump on Jerzy. When he had finished Kyle looked at him. "Plan?" he said.

"I think he needs a change of environment," said Teeny. I've been talking to King Salmon over in hardware. King is due to be promoted, you know."

"Yeah," said Kyle, who knew very well, since his OK was required for any promotion into the ranks of the vice-presidents. "He's gonna get hardware."

"Well, he knows Jerzy pretty well. Thinks he's pretty much an empty suit. Wouldn't be much there if he didn't have all that engineering talent, what there is left of it."

"King thinks Jerzy is an empty suit!" said Kyle, and laughed. "Doesn't say much for us two, since we put Jerzy where he is."

"Jerzy got a little power-hungry is all," said Teeny, grinning.

"So where do we put him?" asked Kyle. "Remember, whatever else he's done, the guy is long-term, and he's always been loyal."

Kyle meant, of course, that Jerzy had always been loyal to Kyle, and that he had been with DataDrive since the very early days. Kyle had a rep for never turning on those who had been with him since the early years, no matter how venal, or stupid, or otherwise ill-adapted to running a large enterprise they might have become.

"Australia," said Teeny.

Kyle reflected for a bit. Australia had been used before as a dumping ground for troublemakers whom he didn't want to fire, either out of considerations of loyalty, or because they simply knew too much and could have been dangerous to DataDrive had they gone over to the enemy.

"What are the Australian numbers?" he asked. "And who's there now?"

"Rusty Mulligan," said Teeny. "The numbers are negligible. This year we'll be lucky to hit fifty mil. That's all in."

"Problem," said Kyle. "It can't be much of a promotion to go from running a division to running a little operation like that."

"We can sell it on futures," said Teeny. "He's our man to develop the vast, untapped potential, etc. etc."

"It won't wash," said Kyle. "I agree Australia's good because they speak English down there, sorta, so the wives don't complain so much. But Jerzy'll never go quietly to a fifty mil geo. What else is near Australia? How about India?"

"Too important," said Teeny. "That really is a future. Naw, if you want to put some sweeteners in there I suggest you throw in Southeast Asia. It's a lot of countries, but not too much business. Of course, we don't want Jerzy running Taiwan. But everything else, let him have it."

"OK," said Kyle.

"Not China, either, though," added Teeny. "I'd better give you a list so you don't give this guy the world!" And both men laughed.

A WEEK LATER, at Kyle's staff, the routine business had been transacted. Toni's promotion to director had been approved with no discussion. Jerzy was then asked to give an impromptu review of where they stood on Nemo. He acquitted himself very well, because he told the truth as he knew it from Chatterjee. Namely that things were looking up, and that a number of technical issues that had held them up seemed to be at the breakthrough stage. Jerzy committed himself to doing a major review of Nemo and two other projects at the staff to be held two weeks hence. He would be the feature presenter at the staff. The timelines were, of course, critical. Jerzy nodded. He understood, if any man did, the importance of Nemo.

Before Jerzy could leave the room Kyle approached him. "Can I see you for a minute?" Jerzy, of course, had no objection to this, and followed Kyle into Kyle's office. Teeny tried to follow them, and Jerzy was secretly tickled to see that Kyle rather abruptly pushed the door closed on him. Jerzy wasn't sure, but he thought he could read a look of consternation on Teeny's moon-shaped face as the door closed.

The two men sat at Kyle's small round table. Jerzy waited patiently. Kyle seemed preoccupied.

Finally Kyle said, "You're doing quite a job with the division." Jerzy started to protest out of modesty, but Kyle held up a hand and said, "No, I mean it, Jerzy. Not every one could have done what you did. And in only eighteen months."

"Thanks, Kyle," said Jerzy, permitting himself a small smile.

"I need your advice," said Kyle, "about a big opportunity we're missing." Jerzy leaned forward and listened attentively. This sounded like an opportunity about to break.

"You've heard of the Asia-Pacific Rim, of course. It's the fastest-growing area in the world. Dozens of countries, all of them booming."

"Right," said Jerzy.

"Right," said Kyle. "But where are we? Where are we in this picture? For example, do you know how much business we did in Australia last year?"

"No, I don't," said Jerzy.

"Fifty mil," said Kyle. "Have you ever heard of Rusty Mulligan?"

"Rusty!" said Jerzy, and his eyes lit up. "Yeah, sure. He's a buddy of mine from way back. He was maybe the second sales person to join up, wasn't he? It was a couple years before I came on board, but everyone knows the job he did."

"Yeah," said Kyle, "well, he's not doing so hot now. He's been running this operation in Australia and New Zealand for two years now, and... zilch!"

"Yeah, well," said Jerzy, "I guess some of the starch went out of old Rusty in recent years."

"I was going to promote him to VP for all of Asia a year ago," said Kyle. "But whaddaya gonna to do with a guy who takes a business over that's doing sixty mil, and after two years he's got it down to fifty mil? I mean!"

"VP for Asia?" said Jerzy, who was beginning to see which way the wind was blowing. "You mean a divisional VP or a corporate VP?" Jerzy was already a divisional VP.

"You gotta be joking!" Kyle said, grinning. "I mean, we're talking maybe half the world's population. India, almost a billion. China, over a billion. Throw in a few of those other countries, jeez, think of the potential!"

"Let me guess," said Jerzy. "You're thinking of reorganizing Asia, putting Japan back in, and running the whole thing out of Hong Kong."

"I'm not talking now," said Kyle, "but you might have something there. And you know, Rusty could've had all this by now, except he couldn't get anything to happen in Australia! Australia, jeez, they speak English down there, don't they? It's not like it's the wilderness. All I needed to go to the Board on the Asia thing was to show that Rusty had some overseas experience. Successful overseas experience."

"Rusty's not the guy," said Jerzy. "Too weak. A good salesman, but as a manager, well..."

"Sort of an empty suit, really," said Kyle.

"You took the words outta my mouth." Jerzy was frantically trying to remember what the Asia numbers were if you folded in Japan. Mostly hardware, of course, but still. King Salmon would know. If he could just get to a phone....

"You know what the total Asia numbers are if we fold in Japan?" asked Kyle, staring at the wall. "I'll tell you. One point three billion."

Jesus! thought Jerzy. That would place Asia, if it were its own business, up there with the major corporations of the U.S. If he were to get control of something that size and run it for a couple of years he could move into any of fifty large corporations as CEO.

"Come to think of it," said Kyle, "maybe what I should do is take a look at making DataDrive Asia an independent company." And he looked at Jerzy. "You ever worked overseas?"

"Ah, no," said Jerzy. "I was in Germany for a year in the Army, is all."

"It's gonna take a year to pull off a geo reorg," said Kyle. "That year could give you time to get the experience I'd need to go to the Board. What do you think?"

Up to now Jerzy had pretty much been going on adrenalin, but now a natural caution took over. "Kyle," he said, "how real is all of this? I mean honestly?"

"As real as anything I've ever planned," said Kyle. "God knows, planning sometimes doesn't seem to mean much in this industry, but I've gotta get our sales to ten billion in five years, and I'm gonna do it, as you know. Asia is one point three now. That's bullshit! I want to double it in three years. How many men can I count on to bring something like this off? I tell you, not many. The only guy besides you I can think of offhand is Salamon."

"King Salmon?" blurted Jerzy.

"Yes."

"Kyle, to be honest, I don't have an answer for you right now about Asia. I mean, it means two moves—one down to Australia for a few months, and then to Hong Kong. I'll have to talk to Lisa, you know. But Kyle, one thing you gotta know. King isn't your man. I know him, in fact we're buddies. I know he started with you before I did, and I'll tell you, he used to be a great salesman, but something happened to the guy. I mean, he's on a constant ego trip. He's turned off customers in Europe—they don't let him roam around over there now without a keeper. I'm not saying this because you're telling me maybe he's for Asia."

"I know that," said Kyle.

"Well, anyway, like I say, I'll talk things over with Lisa, but I'm pretty sure there's not going to be any difficulty there. She's a team player."

"Tell you what," said Kyle. "There's no rush about this. Why don't you take Lisa down there for a week or so? Go to the Great Barrier Reef, take her to the opera in Sydney. Hell, take her to Perth and go sailing! Let her get the feel of the place. You give me the day, I'll have Penelope get you a couple first-class tickets. There's gotta be something cooking down there, this time of year."

"Yeah," said Jerzy, "some conference or other."

"Be sure to stop in Hong Kong," said Kyle. "Real estate is expensive there. Maybe you can make some contacts for us. For when the Board gives us the OK."

"Count on it," said Jerzy. "But I'm just concerned a little about leaving the division for so long. And after I leave, I mean, what's gonna happen to it?"

"Oh, we'll find someone," said Kyle. "The shape you've whipped it into, it's not so important who replaces you."

"Jeez, thanks, Kyle!" said Jerzy, with true delight.

"Later," said Kyle, rising.

FIVE MINUTES AFTER Jerzy had left Teeny showed up. This time he made no effort to enter Kyle's office, but just paused outside, looking in. Kyle looked up and saw him. "Piece of cake," said Kyle.

Teeny nodded and moved on.

# nineteen

I T  H A D  B E E N a quiet night at the headquarters of the Sunnyvale Police. Officer Sanchez had logged in a few problems, but nothing serious so far.

Across from him Lieutenant Weinstock didn't look up as the phone rang. He was working his way through a stack of papers representing work that should have been done a week ago. He heard Officer Sanchez talking but paid no special attention until he heard the word "kidnapping." Then he put down his pencil, shoved his glasses up to his forehead, and looked across the room. Officer Sanchez was taking notes as he listened. Finally Lieutenant Weinstock heard Sanchez saying goodbye to the caller.

"What was that all about?" he said.

"Some lady called and said her son's gone missing. She thinks he's kidnapped. Lives here, name Arthur Smith."

Lieutenant Weinstock sat up, alert now. "A child?"

Officer Sanchez snorted. "Yeah. A thirty-year old child."

The lieutenant relaxed. "So what happened?"

"This lady, her name is Shadroe. Felicia Shadroe. She called from Aspen, Colorado. Said her son flew to San Jose a few days back to report to work at DataDrive. Says he never turned up. The company called, wanted to know where he was."

"She check the house?" asked Lieutenant Weinstock.

"Can't," said Officer Sanchez. "No phone. An apartment a few blocks from here."

"Son got a girlfriend?"

Sanchez yawned. "I asked the lady and she got all ticked off at me. Like I asked did her son have bad breath or something."

"Boyfriend?"

"With an old lady like that he probably never made it to puberty," said Sanchez.

"No fight, no money problem?"

"Nope," said Officer Sanchez. "The guy just dropped out of sight. Thing is, this guy's boss at DataDrive, turns out the mom knows him from some time ago. She calls him and he tells her the guy is working there, he even went to the guy's office and checked it out. Sure enough, the guy's just working away. Then Mom claims the personnel people called her, says the son never showed up. So who ya wanna believe?"

Lieutenant Weinstock considered. "Call someone, have 'em drop over there, see if anything's not kosher. See if someone can get into the place. Sounds like nothing to me, but who knows, these days. You got the mother's phone?"

"Sure, said Officer Sanchez, and he reached over for the radio mike.

AFTER A WHILE the telephone rang. Officer Sanchez answered it.

"Yeah, Joe, let's have it. Yeah? No kidding! What gauge?" There was a long pause during which Officer Sanchez was obviously trying to digest considerable amounts of information. His pencil few across the paper in front of him. Then he said "OK, Joe. See ya," and he put the phone down.

"Imagine that!" he said, half to himself, and half to Lieutenant Weinstock.

"What?" said Lieutenant Weinstock."

"Joe got into the apartment OK. The guy that's supposed to be kidnapped."

"Yeah."

"The super lives on the premises, let him in with no problem. Says he hasn't seen anything of this guy Smith for weeks but that doesn't mean anything, because he never sees anything of Smith. No sign of any funny business in the apartment. No sign of Smith, either, but the guy apparently works all night and sleeps all day, so there's no way to be sure until tomorrow. Unless you want to put a notice out now?"

This last was a question to which Sanchez knew the answer already.

"Sure," grinned the lieutenant. "Let's get an all points out on this fellow. While you're at it, get the Chief of Detectives out of bed and tell him to get his butt over there to dust for prints! What was that guy's name, the guy this Smith works for at DataDrive?"

"Bobochek. Jerzy Bobochek."

"I tell you what, Sanchez. Just in case, you get on the line to DataDrive security, get Bobochek's home number. I'll give him a call. It's not too late."

And when Sanchez had carried out these orders, the Lieutenant found himself speaking with Jerzy. After a quite brief conversation he said, "Thank you, sir. We appreciate your cooperation."

"Sanchez," he said, "if that lady calls again from Aspen you give her to me. Apparently she's pretty wacko. Her son works for Bobochek, who saw him in his office today, and who invites the whole damn Sunnyvale police force to come over tomorrow to check things out."

"I don't think I can make it," said Sanchez.

"Me neither," said the Lieutenant. "By the way, what was that about a shotgun?"

"Shotgun?" said Sanchez.

"Yeah, you were talking to Joe about what gauge the shotgun was, something like that."

Sanchez grinned. "Naw," he said. "No shotgun. This guy Smith is a model railroad freak, like me. He's got a huge layout under construction in the bedroom. HO gauge, you know? The whole thing's apparently hooked up to some kind of computer. I'd like to meet that guy some day."

"Not me," said the Lieutenant.

# twenty

HE HUNT FOR Arthur Smith was delayed a bit for technical reasons. When Fenelon, Chatterjee, and Sandhya reached the San Jose airport they met Sandhya's male friend, Gopal. Sandhya's male friend, as Fenelon found out, was a dentist in real life, but on weekends he was a pilot. Fenelon just could not see Sandhya being attracted to a dentist, good providers though dentists might be. But it was undeniable that women were attracted to pilots, especially pilots who braved the odds and took to the air in very small planes. And Gopal was enough of an experienced pilot to do a nose count, and to calculate that though the Cessna 172 might haul them all to wherever Arthur Smith might be, there would not be sufficient space in the Cessna to bring five persons back. Even if they made themselves very small, Gopal was not going to chance it.

Fenelon, who detested small planes on principle, had to admit a grudging respect for Gopal, even though he hated the way the man laid his eyes on Sandhya from time to time. And that is just what Gopal was doing—laying his eyes heavily on Sandhya, who was dressed for the occasion in form-fitting slacks, a light tan sweater, and a partly unzipped Forty-Niner's windbreaker. Gopal had a dark complexion, was of medium height, sported a moustache which Fenelon had to admit went admirably with the rest of his face, and was a slender, athletic-looking man. He had shaken Fenelon's hand when they had been introduced by Chatterjee, and then had paid him no further attention at all.

Instead, he huddled for a while with Chatterjee, who came over to Arthur and said, "We have a decision to make. The plane is not large enough for the whole party. Either one of us must stay behind, or we must get a different plane."

"Then we'll get a different plane," said Fenelon.

"Yes, but there will be some expense."

"So there will be some expense," said Fenelon, who was beginning to feel a thin wedge of anger entering his heart, or perhaps his gut.

"I see," said Chatterjee, "and of course I agree. I will tell Gopal to rent us the turbocharged plane. It is only a single engine craft, but it has six seats and a lot of power. It will surely get us all safely back."

"I'll pay," said Fenelon.

"No," said Chatterjee, "let us have Arthur Smith pay."

THE TURBOCHARGED AIRCRAFT was noisy. Sandhya sat up front with Gopal, which Fenelon would have resented a great deal, except that she turned frequently and shouted to him and Chatterjee over the roar of the engine. She was enjoying herself, Fenelon saw. Her dark eyes flashed with excitement, and when they hit bumpy air over the Sierras and Fenelon was clinging to a handhold on the side of the cabin to keep from being tossed around, she let out a series of whoops like a child on a rollercoaster.

Chatterjee had plotted their course carefully the day before, but he had done so using only Fenelon's old Rand McNally road atlas, which, it appeared, wasn't at all suitable for guiding the airplane. Gopal had taken nearly an hour to work out how they would get over the Sierras, and then over the other ranges that lay between them and Arthur Smith, reckoning when they would have to land to refuel, and all the time keeping an eye on their destination—a stretch of highway in Western Utah, where Chatterjee felt there was an eighty percent chance of running Arthur to ground.

"Of course, he may be riding at night, since he is used to being awake then. On the other hand it gets extremely cold at night in the high desert, and I cannot imagine Arthur gave much thought to taking suitably warm clothing with him. For one thing, it would be too bulky."

"But on the other hand it gets very hot during the day," said Fenelon. "What person in his right mind would ride a bicycle across a limitless stretch of highway in the midday heat?"

"You have correctly framed the question," said Chatterjee.

"You think Arthur's nuts?" Fenelon asked.

"Not in the usual sense. But I imagine he would greatly benefit by having someone *in loco parentis*, someone with some common sense."

"You mean someone to take Felicia's place," said Fenelon.

"A substitute mother can only go so far," said Chatterjee. "I believe that what Arthur Smith needs is a wife."

"He never thinks of women, I bet."

"Yes, my friend, but that is because he has probably never— how should I say—never known the delights a woman can bring into a lonely man's life."

It was on the tip of Fenelon's tongue to say "And what about you, Chatterjee?" but he said nothing.

They landed at a small field and refueled. Gopal busied himself with the plane, pulling back the engine cover and peering at the engine. He appeared to know what he was doing, and again Fenelon felt admiration and jealousy, all at once. He felt a tugging at his sleeve. It was Sandhya. "Come," she said. "There is a store over there. Help me buy some food."

They walked from the airplane across the grass runway toward a small building at the corner of the field.

"This is wonderful fun, isn't it!" said Sandhya.

"Great fun," said Fenelon, who at that moment was wishing that he and Sandhya were walking somewhere in Mountain View.

"Come, now! Don't be a killjoy," she said. "We will find Arthur Smith, make a nice picnic, fly back, and then..."

"And then what?"

"Well, we will see. Here we are. Gopal is a vegetarian. I hope they have something for him."

IT WAS THE next morning. They had started at eight, and had been in the air for about ninety minutes, flying at an altitude of about a thousand feet. Enough, as Chatterjee had said, to give them some scope, but low enough so they wouldn't miss a bicyclist. They followed the state highway, which was almost devoid of traffic of any kind. There was no talking now. Each one was scanning the road below.

Fenelon hadn't slept well at the cheap motel, but it was the only place for two hundred miles around that had an airstrip next to it. The bed had been too soft, and his back was sore. There had been only two beds in the room, a queensize and a twinsize. Chatterjee took possession of the twinsize as soon as they entered the room, posing his little knapsack on the covers, and sitting down on the mattress to remove his shoes.

Gopal and Fenelon had stared at each other with considerable antipathy. Either they would have to share the queensize bed, an idea which Fenelon, at least, found extremely distasteful, or they would have to toss to see who would sleep on the floor. Gopal had said "I will be happy to sleep on the floor. I can use the chair cushion as a pillow." Then he had looked at Fenelon expectantly. But all Fenelon had said was "All right," and had immediately thrown himself onto the queensize bed and closed his eyes.

Sandhya had a room to herself, of course, and had come into the little coffee shop the next morning looking like an Eastern princess, Fenelon thought. She had put her hair up, and although she had on a blue denim skirt and a white blouse, Fenelon saw no contradiction between this attire and the image of an Eastern princess. She giggled when Gopal had complained about sleeping on the floor. But then she had reached out and squeezed Gopal's wrist, and had thanked him for his invaluable help. Gopal had smiled then, and had yawned sensuously, turning his head decorously away, but leaving his wrist in Sandhya's grasp.

Fenelon had felt a pang of jealousy. Or something stronger, if possible. The thing that bothered him was that Gopal had evidently been part of Sandhya's life for a long time. They seemed to be on very close terms. But how could any man be close to a woman like Sandhya for a long time without doing something about it? Had Gopal strung her along, perhaps promising marriage, but not just yet? He looked like a playboy. And Fenelon had always thought that Indian women married very young. Perhaps Sandhya had been married, and her husband had died, and she had come to America to escape having to die herself on his funeral pyre. But no, that practice had surely gone out of style.

Now they were flying above Utah. This morning Chatterjee had taken a pair of field glasses out of his knapsack, and was now seated next to Gopal, who had taken the plane to the left side of the highway. Chatterjee had pushed the window back to get a better view, and the cold air rushed about the cabin. Fenelon shivered, and looked over at Sandhya. She was shivering, too. He had an intense desire to reach out and hold her hand. She was looking at a distant range of mountains to her left—there was, of course, no way that she could see the highway. Fenelon gazed at her neck, the back of her head crowned by the coil of black hair, her slim arms resting in her lap. Gopal was intent on flying the plane. Chatterjee was scanning the highway with the binoculars.

Fenelon reached out and put his hand over hers. Sandhya turned to him. She smiled, and Fenelon felt his heart begin to thump wildly. He was like a schoolboy, but he couldn't help it, and didn't care.

They looked at each other for a long moment. Fenelon had just begun to lean toward her when there came a cry from Chatterjee.

"There he is!"

There didn't seem to be much doubt about it. Who else would be pedaling along a hundred miles from nowhere? Gopal circled and brought the plane down to no more than a hundred feet. The cyclist looked up in alarm. He was blonde, and wore what looked like plaid Bermuda shorts and a white polo shirt. The bicycle had panniers on the front, and saddle bags on the rear.

"We'll land over there!" shouted Gopal, pointing to a field about a mile away. "If it is solid, that is."

"Land on the highway!" cried Sandhya. "No one is coming."

"Only in an emergency!" replied Gopal. "That can be big trouble."

"The road!" squawked Chatterjee excitedly, the fieldglasses dangling now from his neck. "The road!"

And so it was on the road that Arthur Smith found them five minutes later. And, of course, Chatterjee got in the first word as the sweating, sunburned cyclist rode up to them. "Mr. Arthur Smith, I presume?"

IT WAS GENERALLY agreed that it would be better to get the airplane into the air as soon as possible. It was almost incredible that twenty minutes had passed without even a pickup truck coming their way. But as Chatterjee observed, most traffic was likely to take the divided highway several miles to the South.

What was even more incredible was the amount of information that Arthur Smith seemed able to absorb without showing either astonishment or dismay. Not even the knowledge that in the last four weeks an impostor had been receiving his paychecks seemed to impress him. In fact, he seemed to manifest little emotion of any kind until Fenelon had concluded his part of the saga with the phrase "so you see, Arthur, you've got to get to DataDrive as soon as possible and take your rightful place, as it were."

At that, Arthur had looked up sharply and then had shaken his head. "Nope," he said. "No way."

"No way what?" said Fenelon, with a sinking feeling.

"I'm getting out of software," Arthur said. "I've been thinking hard for the last few days, and I'm going to make a change. I want to open a bike shop."

"Dear Arthur," said Chatterjee gently, while Fenelon gazed unseeing along the road. "I believe that is a good decision. It so happens that I have relatives in the business. Not that they would take you in, of course, but they could help you learn your way around the suppliers, get a feel of the market, that sort of thing."

"I don't think I need any of that," said Arthur, as he patted his bicycle's handlebars with affection.

"We will talk about it in the airplane," Chatterjee said suavely. "I would also like to tell you one or two problems I have encountered with a certain project, a very important project to me and to Data-Drive.

"You mean Nemo?" asked Arthur, and his eyes lit up just a bit.

"So much for corporate security," said Chatterjee with a laugh.

It was a short while later that they discovered that the bicycle would not fit into the airplane. The front wheel could be detached, and that went into the rear of the cabin quite handily; but the frame would not fit, even after the handlebars had been turned down. Arthur and Fenelon reassembled the bicycle, while Chatterjee surveyed them musingly.

"Well, he said finally, "the choices are plain. Either we leave the bicycle here, well hidden, of course, and send someone back for it, or" he added hastily, seeing a frown starting to creep over Arthur's face, "or we have someone ride it back," and he looked meaningfully at Fenelon, whose hands were black from grease and road dirt that had accumulated on the bicycle chain.

It was not until Chatterjee had explained to Arthur that Fenelon had been a great cyclist in his younger days, and in fact had been a member of the famous All-Indiana men's racing team, and that he cared for bicycles more than for life itself, that Arthur entrusted his Peugeot to Fenelon and got into the plane, guided by Chatterjee, who had reached up to place a large hand on Arthur's shoulder, and was clearly not going to remove it until Arthur was safely stowed aboard. Gopal was in the pilot's seat. Chatterjee and Arthur were in the second row. Clearly Sandhya was going to travel next to Gopal for the next few hours, Fenelon reflected bitterly.

Then he became aware that Sandhya had come over to him and was standing in front of him. She reached for his hand and gripped it tightly.

"Thank you, Fenelon," she said softly. "Having Arthur with him will be a great help to my brother. I hope you will come to dinner next week. As soon as you return."

"Well, I'll probably take a shower first," Fenelon said.

Sandhya laughed. "Please do. My auntie will be in Los Angeles for ten days. Chatterjee, of course, will be working in the labs. I am sure he is wondering how long he can hold Arthur's attention."

"I'm sure your brother will have Arthur by his side for as long as he wants," said Fenelon with feeling. "That guy could charm the birds out of the trees. The All-Indiana men's racing team!"

"I will be alone," said Sandhya, "so I hope the prospect of dinner with only me will not discourage you."

"Er, no" said Fenelon.

"Of course," Sandhya went on, smiling, "I could invite friends over. To make it easier for you. In terms of conversation, I mean."

"Ah, no, I think it would be nice, just the two of us," said Fenelon.

"It is very untraditional and daring," she said. "You know how conservative we Indians are."

"Yes," said Fenelon. "We can just have a nice talk."

"You can ask me what it is I do," said Sandhya.

"I know what you do, said Fenelon. "You're a CPA. I thought maybe we could push the conversation a bit further."

"Maybe we could," she said, as the engine of the plane coughed twice and then sputtered into life.

Chatterjee stuck his head out the window. "Come on," he yelled. "Gopal has patients this afternoon."

# twenty-one

Dear Emile,

*Thanks for your card from the Carlsbad Caverns. I'm glad to see that you were out and about on your vacation, though I think it would be good for you to get above ground more!*

*It was gratifying to see that the Postal Service was able to get my letter to you within ten days. Here in the Valley everyone uses E-mail, which is all done by computer, and messages get where they're going in the twinkling of an eye. Imagine what would have happened if Madame de Sévigné had had access to E-mail! The literary salons would have become video arcades.*

*Let me tell you, though, in E-mail not much attention is paid to the niceties of literary style. If I were a teacher of composition, and were correcting some of the E-mails I've got, there wouldn't be a letter low enough in the alphabet to represent a fair grade. One of the most amusing orthographic elements is that any time an "s" is tacked onto a word, the E-mail author seems compelled to insert an apostrophe between it and the main word. Well, I'm exaggerating a bit, but it seems that way. Adverbs have also been done away with. Also, friendships and working relationships have been ruined by intemperate messages sent in the heat of battle, so to speak. I mean, once you've pulled the trigger there's no calling the bullet back. No leisurely walk to the mailbox, during which time you might reflect on the wisdom of what you're about to send someone. Here the pace of life is just too fast.*

*Well, I have a lot to tell you. The biggest news is about the return of Arthur Smith. Well, actually, that's not the biggest news (you see, if this were E-mail I could have just wiped out what I wrote and this letter would be more coherent than it is). But Arthur Smith is big news, anyway. We snatched him from the bosom of Mother Earth, so to speak, and bore him triumphant through the skies like Phoebus Apollo bearing the sun in his chariot. Or whatever the Greeks thought. In fact, I wasn't actually in the chariot. I had to ride Arthur's bicycle back to Sunnyvale, California, from a very desolate spot somewhere in the desert. Thank heavens I was well equipped with sandwiches, though most were of the vegetarian persuasion. I can tell you, when you are riding an old Peugeot bicycle over the Sierras you want something more substantial than sprouts and nine-grain bread.*

*I'm exaggerating, of course. I had some money and was able to refuel, so to speak, at various eateries along the way. For the first time in my adult life I didn't feel guilty eating pizza with extra cheese. I must have burned several thousand calories a day, and was able to recapture my svelte figure from the Kachina chip god.*

*I was rather sorry that my route didn't take me anywhere near Winnemucca, Nevada. Not for any reason other than seeing Joey and the gang again. So far as the other stuff is concerned, I'm a changed man. Which is part of the really big story. But let me first get back to Arthur....*

# twenty-two

ARTHUR SMITH ARRIVED at DataDrive in a taxi. He would have preferred waiting for his bicycle to arrive and just talk with Chatterjee about Nemo over caffè latte and scones, but Chatterjee had told him that he, Chatterjee, could only hold so much caffè latte, and that anyway, more than two glasses of it made him nervous and jumpy. Arthur wasn't very good at assessing people's behavior patterns, but he did comprehend that Chatterjee did not need more nervous energy than he already possessed. Talking with Arthur at Arthur's residence was out of the question, since Arthur had only one chair, which he lugged from the kitchen to the model train room as need dictated. Chatterjee was not comfortable sitting on floors, or even on futons, unless they were rolled up and against a wall. And so Arthur had to present himself at DataDrive, which he did two days after returning to California, and just as Fenelon was beginning the long uphill battle across the Sierra Nevada.

Chatterjee was in the taxi with Arthur, just to make sure that the driver got paid the correct amount, and to give Arthur an encouraging shove, if necessary. For a moment he had considered whether he should accompany Arthur into the lobby of Building Fifteen, but decided that it wouldn't be advisable as yet for the two of them to be seen together. So he descended with Arthur, but walked across the street to visit some of his team in Building Two. (Little in the way of urban planning had gone into the layout of the DataDrive buildings, and, as with street numbers in Tokyo, the numbers of the buildings had no discernable relationship to their location.)

Arthur went into Building Fifteen just as Carmelita came out. She didn't pay him any attention, because she was deciding when and where she would like to have Kurt propose to her. She was also wondering about her family's reaction. Her father's brother, Fidelio, was fiercely proud of his Hispanic heritage, and might feel hurt, or even angry, once he learned that his niece Carmelita was going to marry a gringo. Fidelio owned a collection of weapons, including two machetes and a short-barreled .32 revolver. The machetes were kept in a shed behind the house and hadn't been used in years. Carmelita imagined that they must have become quite rusty, and she couldn't see Fidelio rescuing the family's honor with a rusty machete.

The .32 revolver, on the other hand, was in excellent condition. Carmelita knew this because Fidelio brought it out every New Year's Eve and cleaned and oiled and loaded it, so that he could shoot it off in the air just as the Old Year ended and the New Year began. It was a tradition in the neighborhood, and one that the local police force would have liked to suppress. At about one minute after midnight each New Year's Day, a rain of bullets would come down on the neighborhood and surrounding areas, one of which was largely settled by Koreans. The Koreans did not celebrate their New Year at the same time as the Hispanics, and certainly not with the same exuberance. In 1989 an ethnic conflict had been narrowly avoided, but only because the women of both the Korean and Hispanic camps had risen and disarmed the men. This had so shocked the men that in 1990 a sullen peace had reigned, with only a desultory slug or two coming to earth here and there, with a loud snap. But that was some time ago, and things had slipped back into their old pattern.

Trudi was knitting away. The phone hadn't gurgled for a while, so she did hear the faint sound of Arthur clearing his throat. When she looked up she saw a sunburned, plumpish and serious face looking down at her. He wasn't a knockout, that was for sure, but he was kind of nice-looking, she thought. His hair was blond and hung down over his forehead.

"How can I help you?"

"I'm Arthur Smith. I'm here to see Toni Hunter."

Trudi smiled, and Arthur smiled back. Trudi thought that when he smiled he really looked pretty good. She said "You're not lost? I thought you must be looking for some address."

"I am," said Arthur. "This one. This is DataDrive Building Fifteen, isn't it?"

"Oh yes," said Trudi. "Do you have an appointment with Toni?"

"Not really," said Arthur. "But I think she'll see me.

"Did you say your name was Arthur Smith?" asked Trudi. "We have an Arthur Smith who works right here in this building."

"I know," said Arthur.

"You do?" said Trudi, with a stare. "He's not a relation, is he?"

"No connection," said Arthur. "By the way, what is your name?"

"Trudi," said Trudi, and she felt the blush begin to rise.

"Trudi what?"

"Schmidthals. Trudi Schmidthals."

"Schmidthals," repeated Arthur, and Trudi noticed that he pronounced it correctly. "Trudi is a pretty name."

"It's short for Gertrude, which is not a pretty name," said Trudi.

"Who says?" said Arthur, smiling again.

"I don't like it," said Trudi. "I've never liked it."

"Then I'll just use Trudi," said Arthur.

"Are you here to be interviewed?" Trudi asked. "Toni is director of recruiting. It would be confusing to have two employees in the same building with the same name."

"You won't have that problem," said Arthur, and Trudi's face fell.

"So you're not going to be interviewed?"

"I've already been interviewed. In fact, I was hired a few weeks ago. I have a badge, but I can't get to it for a few days. Also, it's got the wrong photo on it."

"I'm a little lost," said Trudi.

"Well, I will try to tell you as much as I know, which isn't all that much. But right now I think I should see Miss Hunter."

"Call her Toni," said Trudi. "She doesn't like the Miss part much."

"Do you work here all the time?" asked Arthur.

"No, I'm what they call a floater. I fill in for the receptionists when they go on break or have lunch. I'm just a temp."

"Do you ever have lunch?" asked Arthur.

"I usually bring it from home," Trudi said. "Saves money, you know. I need every penny I can get. For school."

"Maybe when I'm through here we can go get something to eat," said Arthur. "Though I don't drive, and I don't know what's around here."

"I have a car," said Trudi slowly. "It's just an old bug, and sometimes it doesn't even start and I have to kind of kick it."

"I can fix bugs," said Arthur, and again he smiled. "Lunch will be on me." And now Trudi felt her control slipping, and her heart started to beat pretty strongly.

TONI HUNTER DIDN'T know who had taken the photos of her and Fenelon through the mail slot in Arthur Smith's office. It was just as well, or she might have found it impossible to be in the lobby at the same time as Carmelita. So she didn't feel any particular relief that it was Trudi, not Carmelita, who called her to say that there was another Arthur Smith waiting for her in the lobby. Toni was a director now, and didn't feel that she should have to walk downstairs to meet Arthur. She would much rather have had Trudi bring him up, but of course receptionists never left their stations unless they were covered. And Daphne was out ill. So Toni went down to the lobby.

It is a credit to her years of HR experience that she instantly spotted how things were, and were likely to develop, between Arthur and Trudi. The two of them were looking at each other, Arthur hanging over the counter, his head within a few inches of Trudi. He was so close to her that Toni didn't see how his eyes could focus, unless he was myopic. And it is to her further credit that, though Arthur was fairly attractive, she didn't for a moment entertain unworthy thoughts of anything other than a professional relationship. She was a director, after all.

Since the processing of Arthur Smith into the ranks of Data-Drive had already taken place, the meeting was *pro forma*, to use Toni's phrase. The only real issue was how to get a new badge for Arthur. The photos were in color, and there was just no way that Fenelon's dark mop could be confused with Arthur's golden locks.

"It's a no-brainer, really," Toni said. "We'll just tell Security that Arthur's badge was lost. I mean, the other Arthur's badge. You'll go over and they'll take another photo of you, and that'll be that."

And it was just that easy. Arthur had his new badge that very morning, and could come and go freely. Toni escorted him to his offices. He had admired everything, especially the futon. And he had made an attempt to fire up C3, but Toni quickly pulled him away. She wanted to introduce him to the head of a very important project. She found Chatterjee alone in his office, introduced him to Arthur Smith, and then left the two software gurus alone.

"How are things?" said Chatterjee.

"Going very well," said Arthur.

"Did you see the stack of stuff on your shelf? It's all about Nemo, but most of it is crap," said Chatterjee. "There is no other word. I have to start in two or three new directions, as we discussed on the plane. The problem is that we only have the resources for one direction. If you don't mind, I will show you something. Let me call it up," and he turned to his computer.

"Do you have an alarm clock?" asked Arthur. "I need to meet someone for lunch at one o'clock. She is picking me up, so I have to be outside."

Chatterjee turned to look at him. "I see," he said. "Anyone I know?"

Arthur blushed through the tan. "It's the receptionist."

Chatterjee sat a little straighter. "You mean Carmelita? The dark-haired one?"

"No," said Arthur, "Trudi. The pretty blonde one."

"I am relieved," said Chatterjee. "You are very perceptive. Trudi is quiet, but quite smart. She is studying to be a chemist, I believe."

"Is that so?" said Arthur. "Chemistry was my major in college."

"Is that so?" said Chatterjee. "Well, it sounds as if fate is playing around."

"It's only lunch," said Arthur, blushing. "Remember in the airplane you talked to me about, what was it... getting anchored, or something? I think that Trudi would make a nice anchor. I mean, she works here, right in the building. And she doesn't know anything at all about software. So it's sort of like what you were recommending. Remember?"

"Indeed," said Chatterjee.

Arthur's face grew somber. "You know, she has been working to pay her way through college, and she is only a temp. Each quarter she isn't sure whether she'll still have a job. If she was full-time she'd have a little more security, at least. And the company might even pay some of her tuition."

"Only if her program of study fits the company's requirements," said Chatterjee. "Remember, she is neither a business major nor a computer science major. She is studying chemistry."

"Well, being a chem major didn't stop me," said Arthur with some feeling.

"You are quite correct, Arthur," said Chatterjee. "I propose a deal with you. You commit to stay here in the labs at DataDrive at least through the end of this calendar year. In turn, I will tell you how Trudi can become a full-time employee. That would please you, isn't it so?"

"Sure," said Arthur. "It's a deal."

"Very well, here is what you will do. You will pick up the telephone right now and call Ms. Toni Hunter. If she is not there you can leave her a voicemail message. You will tell her that there is one small favor you desire from her. That is that Trudi shall become a full-time employee of security. No, wait! Better than that, a half-time admin at DataDrive. With flex hours. That way she can control her time a bit more. The money will be about the same, and if she works twenty hours or more a week, and has a badge, the tuition reimbursement program is possible.

"And if Toni says no?" asked Arthur.

Chatterjee grinned. "Please just tell her I suggested it. I am sure she will cooperate. And as soon as you get that out of the way we can get down to real business."

# twenty-three

**J**ERZY BOBOCHEK WAS preparing for his get-acquainted trip to Australia with Lisa, his young and beautiful wife, so he didn't review the agenda for Sammi's quarterly all-hands meeting. It wasn't until he was already at the hotel where the meeting was to take place—DataDrive had grown so large that there was no company meeting room large enough for everyone—that he took a glance at the E-mail his admin had printed out for him giving the order of events. He saw that Sammi intended to introduce Arthur Smith as a new employee.

Normally the names of new employees were read out at the all-hands meetings; each person was asked to stand, and then the group was given a round of welcoming applause. Jerzy saw that Arthur Smith was the only new employee his division had hired over the last quarter. This was good news to him, as he knew for a fact that about thirty employees had left the division to take their skills elsewhere, which meant that the division was that much leaner and meaner. And lean and mean was the name of the game. Jerzy felt that, all in all, he could leave the division in pretty good shape to whomever Kyle saw fit to offer it. That was important, because Jerzy had definitely decided to take the Asia-Pacific job, starting in Australia. He had had a drink or two with King Salmon, who was clearly totally unaware that Kyle had had thoughts of offering him the job. King had been more than usually thoughtful.

"You know, Jerzy, it's a great opportunity for you. Rusty Mulligan, I mean if you can't double the business from what he's been doing, why, hell's bells."

Jerzy had to agree with this sentiment.

"Another thing," King had said. "This outfit you belong to, the Sons of Liberty."

"Firebrands," Jerzy had corrected him.

"I'll bet Australia could be fertile territory for them," said King. "You saw Crocodile Dundee a few years ago, didn't you?"

Jerzy had seen this film.

"That's the way most Australians are, like Paul what's-his-name. Rugged, carry big knives, ready for anything. Make pretty good recruits if given the right leadership."

"Of course, I'd only be there a few months," said Jerzy. "I'm not sure what you can do with a bunch of Aussies in just a few months."

"Time enough to get things started," said King.

Jerzy thought he might have something there, but he didn't want to give King anything to use against him, so he just said, "Well, I'll pretty much have my hands full turning things around. Probably have to can a few people."

"Yeah, you'll have to go down and kick some butt," said King, using the debonair expression then current in the industry. And they had a few more drinks.

At the hotel all was bustle and excitement as the HR staff assigned to such events rushed around, making sure that the food and drink were ready to be put out on the long trestle tables in the corridors adjoining the Grand Ballroom, where the meeting was to take place. They also checked the electrical connections to be sure there would be no repeat of the embarrassing episode of two quarters ago, when the mike had failed just when Sammi was delivering the punch line of a very clever joke he had thought of all by himself. And they had to be sure the hotel's expensive multimedia equipment was set up to deliver the full-color video of Kyle's remarks, which would be projected onto a huge screen at the front of the ballroom. That was always the high point of the quarterly all-hands.

Jerzy mingled with some of the other bigwigs in a corner of the ballroom, which had been half-darkened. He traded friendly insults with Teeny, who was going to be delivering some remarks on how the competition was doing. Teeny clapped him on the shoulder. No one, of course, knew that in about a year he, Jerzy, would be the CEO of DataDrive Asia-Pacific, Inc. It made Jerzy feel really important to have such a secret under his belt. Lisa, of course, had been impressed, even stunned by the news that this was in the works. She was at Nordstrom's this very minute trying to see what she could buy that would go with the Great Barrier Reef and its social life.

In the penumbra of the ballroom Jerzy was not able to see Felicia Shadroe enter through a rear door and sit down on a folding chair against the wall. Felicia had given up on the Sunnyvale Police Department. She had flown in that morning and had tried to get into Arthur's apartment to see if he were really living there, but the super, who was mindful of the interest the police had taken in Arthur not so very long ago, had rudely refused her entry, even after she had shown her driver's license, and then threatened him with exposure as a left-leaning closet homo. Then Felicia had taken the cab, which had waited patiently for her at the curb, to Data-Drive, where she demanded to be admitted to the labs. Carmelita was on duty and had instantly sized her up as a crazy. The full day of training each receptionist had received upon being hired dealt with crazies in a special fifteen-minute segment. The instructions were simple. Speak calmly, smile a lot, and dial 666. This was a special code that would bring reinforcements but fast.

That was what had happened. Carmelita had calmly informed

Felicia that everyone was at a meeting at the Temblor Hotel in Palo
Alto, and that if Felicia would just sit down for a few hours, she
could see her son when he returned. Unfortunately, Felicia had
become so infuriated at Carmelita's constant smiling that she had
cursed her and rushed out of the building and left in the cab
moments before three white security jeeps rolled up, two driven by
men, and one by a woman. Each of these persons was qualified in
Okinawan karate, and as Carmelita observed later to Trudi, it
would have been interesting to see who came out on top, Felicia or
Okinawa.

Felicia's cab driver was a quiet man from the Philippines who
spent his evenings in Daly City, in a house that was almost his, and
he didn't want any trouble. So when he finally got Felicia to the
hotel where the quarterly meeting was about to begin he told her
he had heard on his radio that his daughter was hemorrhaging in a
hospital emergency room and he had to rush to her side. Felicia
thrust some bills at him and he immediately drove off.

IT WAS GETTING harder and harder to get employees excited
about the all-hands meetings. Sometimes it seemed to Sammi that
the only people to get really up for them were the HR people.  Just
as the Roman emperors were constantly forced to improve on the
games in the Coliseum to keep the mob content, adding a few more
Christians here, a few more wild beasts there, and probably remov-
ing any restrictions on the sale of alcoholic beverages for the occasion, so Sammi felt obligated to add a few fillips to each successive
all-hands quarterly.

Sammi had not undertaken classical studies, so he didn't know
much about the Roman games, and may even have been totally
ignorant that they ever took place. The only way he could have
known about the subject would have been through a few old
Hollywood films. But Caligula, Nero and the rest of them would
have been proud at the way the agendas for these meetings were
carefully constructed to build interest and tension.

True, Sammi did not eliminate any Christians. At the most, he mutilated a few of the more unusual names when he had to read off the lists of top performers and teams that had won awards. Sammi was simply not able to wrap his tongue around Xien Chuang Li, or Veeraswamy Ramachandran, each of whom had won prizes at the last quarterly. As for Ferdozi Schwarma Mukhtar, he was still inwardly seething at Sammi six months after Sammi had tried three times to pronounce his name and had finally given up, calling him "Ferdi." Ferdozi had, thank God, dissuaded his uncle, who was an imam of some note, from issuing a *fatwa* against Sammi.

One of the big pulls for the employees at these meetings was the food and drink, which were plentiful and good. You didn't get the food and drink, however, unless you sat through the meeting, because the food and drink were laid on in the North Corridor, and the employees were only admitted to the South Corridor before the all-hands began. There they milled about like cattle in a feeding lot. When the doors of the ballroom were opened and they could at last enter, some of the hungrier employees would always try rushing across to the doors that led to the North Corridor. But their way was blocked by some of the more stalwart HR folks, and they had to return to be seated.

Another big pull was the raffle. At the end of each quarterly various prizes were raffled off. You didn't have to buy a ticket, because the HR folks had prepared a big basket of slips of paper, each slip bearing a badge number. All you had to do was to be present and have your number called to win. If you were out of town on business Sammi would call for a vote, which was always an amusing event in itself. No one ever won a raffle if he or she weren't present, because the crowd of employees would always whistle and hoot until a new badge number was drawn. This was probably the closest the all-hands meeting actually came to the games the Romans used to hold in the Coliseum.

In the early days the prizes weren't of great value. Maybe a dinner for two in a local Thai restaurant, or an overnight at some motel in Carmel-by-the-Sea. And there weren't so many of them.

In recent times, though, what with morale depressed by the situation in the industry, and the notion that each employee was, after all, just an entrepreneur who happened to be working for a time at this particular company, Sammi had felt it advisable to up the value of the raffle, and thus ensure a full turnout each time.

The all-hands meetings were part of Sammi's MBOs, which meant that he was going to do them even if he had to give away ten new BMWs to get people to show. And so the overnight at Carmel-by-the-Sea developed into four nights at a luxurious resort on Kauai. The local Thai restaurant meal for two became dinner for two at the Ritz Carleton in San Francisco, with a cozy room and a chilled bottle of genuine French champagne waiting just upstairs. And so on.

The problem, of course, was that there was no end in sight. The employees' expectations had been tuned to an ever-increasing rain of valuable prizes. The budget was beginning to creak under the strain. It was a problem Sammi intended to hand over to Toni Hunter.

THE MEETING HAD begun. The video of Kyle had gone over pretty well. It had featured Kyle dressed in a gorilla suit, trying to get the competition's systems to work by squashing them with bananas. During the video a small, smartly-dressed woman with a lacquered hairdo could have been seen scuttling up and down the aisles, peering down each row as though looking for someone. But everyone was too busy laughing at Kyle's antics to notice.

Now all the VPs got up on the stage and stood in a semicircle, getting ready for the performance awards. Each employee getting a performance award got a plaque, a check, and got to have his picture taken with the VPs. But first, it was traditional to introduce the new employees. Sammi started with the new admins, and Trudi, blushing beet red, had to stand up and was warmly applauded. She sat down with relief, reaching out for Arthur's hand and squeezing it a bit before letting go. Then came the introductions of the new sales and marketing people, the operations people, and the finance and legal people. There were maybe twenty-five in all, so it didn't take long.

Then Sammi held up his hand. "Before we get to the new hires in the software development group, I want to make an announcement about the group."

Jerzy looked at Sammi with amazement. An announcement? About his group? This wasn't on his copy of the agenda.

"You all know what a great job Jerzy has done with the group," said Sammi. "And so I know you'll share my pleasure when I announce that Jerzy has been promoted."

A great hush filled the hall.

"Jerzy will be leaving in a few weeks to take on new responsibilities as the head of our Australia/New Zealand operations," said Sammi, "and he will..." but his words were drowned out by a rising cheer that seemed to go on and on. Sammi looked back at Jerzy with a wide smile, put his hand over the mike, and shouted over the din "They really love ya, guy!" Jerzy smiled weakly, and in response to the enthusiasm of the audience gave a little wave. He had not thought that Kyle wanted the news to get out just yet, and of course because Sammi's words had been drowned out, the employees hadn't yet learned that his initial responsibilities included not only the lands Down Under, but also most of Asia as well. He waited patiently for Sammi to complete the announcement.

But when the noise finally died away Sammi merely said, "And now, our last new employee, who is, of course, in the software division. I'm very pleased to announce that we've stolen Arthur Smith away from the clutches of Siegfried Software. Arthur, as some of you know, has been a regular contributor of technical articles to the top industry publications and is a valued member of the DataDrive team working on an important project. Stand up, Arthur! Hey, you guys over there, get a light on Arthur, will ya, so folks'll know who he is."

Arthur did not want to stand, but Trudi, exercising for the first time the powerful and beneficial influence that she would have over Arthur for the rest of his life, put her hand under his arm and pushed him up. He stood up just as a bright light hit him smack in the face, and just as Felicia turned from the row opposite where she had been seeking him in vain. Giving a little maternal cry she trotted over to him and flung her arms around his neck, giving him a long hug and a prolonged kiss.

The applause for Arthur, which had been desultory at best, since engineers do not like to have someone singled out for honor without having proved himself on their home field, rose sharply and became a chorus of cries and shrieks. To most of the audience, who were not close enough to see that Felicia was old enough to be his mother, it appeared as if some female employee had suddenly gone berserk and was sexually assaulting him. There was envy in their breasts, but they were sporting enough to cheer, the men for Arthur, the women for Felicia.

Those immediately adjacent to the couple were confused, but thought it best to join in the general expression of joy. Sammi Boydjian stared out at what seemed to be pandemonium, as the semicircle of VPs behind him smiled and clapped dutifully, unaware that this was not in the script. No one heard the plaintive voice of Jerzy Bobochek, who was saying, half aloud and half to himself, "That's not Arthur Smith."

As Arthur disengaged himself from his mother and looked around for the nearest exit, he felt Trudi standing next to him. She put her arm protectively around him and he could feel her body pressing against his. Trudi stuck her other arm out and grabbed Felicia's free hand, the one that was not dabbing at her eyes with a tissue. Trudi had understood all. "Hello, Mrs. Smith," she had said. "I'm Trudi Schmidthals."

Felicia stared at Trudi. The noise was dying down, and folks were starting to think of the food and drink, and were casting longing glances at the doors to the North corridor. Felicia tried to speak but she was so overcome by the sight of Arthur with Trudi's arm firmly around him that all she could say was "It's not Smith. It's Shadroe."

It was one of the most succcessful all-hands meetings ever. All hands were agreed on that point.

# twenty-four

**F**ENELON WAS GETTING tired of bicycling across the Central Valley. Alhough he was normally full of admiration for the inventive genius of the French, he could not see how they could have produced a bicycle that grew heavier with every mile. And yet he had to admit that the Peugeot had stood up admirably under the strain of the trip. It had been five days since he had said goodbye to the aeronauts, and he had had two spills, which had wrought some considerable damage to his left elbow and the palm of his right hand, but which had left the Peugeot relatively unscathed. He was beginning to eliminate from his future plans any ideas about becoming a farmer. Endless rows of legumes were succeeded by endless fields of fruit trees, and these were in turn succeeded by endless brown meadows which seemed simply to have been put there to illustrate his isolation.

Arthur Smith had provided himself with three plastic water bottles which appeared to hold about a quart each. Fenelon's first practical task was to augment these at a friendly vegetable stand with two gallon-size plastic jugs, which he filled with water and tied to the frame of the Peugeot with some clothesline. In one of the saddlebags he found a large cotton hat, which was useful in delaying, at the very least, the toxic effect of the merciless sun.

He had discovered that the best system for covering immense distances was to avoid looking at the horizon, and instead to look down at the particular section of the road he was traveling over at the moment. That way he had at least the illusion of forward movement. But it was keeping his head down that had led to the two spills. In the first accident he had run into a large rock. The Peugeot had stopped, water jugs describing wild arcs through the air at the end of the bits of clothesline. Fenelon himself had continued the journey for a few feet.

The second accident was caused by the sudden appearance at Fenelon's feet of a large and determinedly unfriendly farm dog of uncertain ancestry, and with little regard for bicyclists. The dog had seemed quite content to have caused him to crash, and had simply stood there and surveyed the effect of his eruption into Fenelon's life. He didn't even snarl at Fenelon, and Fenelon did not dare to snarl at him. After a while the dog had simply wandered away, back to the yard of the farmhouse.

These incidents had caused Fenelon to become philosophical, which is always a dangerous state of mind when one is faced with a Herculean task. The best thing would have been to suspend all normal thought processes and become an automaton, simply pedaling up and down, perhaps counting to oneself until one reached a million or so. Instead, Fenelon began to think about all the things that had crowded into his life in the last few months. At the beginning of this process, of course, that involved thinking about Antje and the children. Fenelon was aware that, for once, he wasn't thinking about them in the sense of judging them, or himself with respect to them, or in the sense of planning to do anything. Instead, he was just thinking about them. He was running old videos in his mind, calling up this scene or that one at will.

Rather than become involved in a third, and possibly serious mishap with the Peugeot, Fenelon pulled off the road and wheeled the bicycle under a large, leafy tree that was one of sixty thousand or so in this particular field. It was loaded with oranges or pomelos, or some other kind of citrus fruit. Fenelon was too tired to investigate at the moment, and he was beginning to feel somewhat disheartened. He propped the Peugeot against the trunk of the tree, untied one of the plastic gallon jugs, and took a long draft of warm water, then moved a few steps away and urinated. As he did so he realized that he had not once thought of his prostate in the last four or five weeks. Even now that he was thinking about not having thought about it, it didn't seem all that important.

He returned to the tree, sat down with his back against the trunk, and started running video clips again. There was the receptionist at Building Fifteen, directing him to the men's room. And Toni Hunter, proudly escorting him to her office to induct him into the mysteries of the high tech world. Chatterjee appeared, grinning, and telling him about the Ramayana, the story of Prince Rama and his beautiful consort, Princess Sita, who closely resembled Sandhya. There were no computers in those days, of course. So how had Rama and his brother, the fierce Lakshmana, organized the army to invade and defeat the evil demon king, Rawanna? Armies required masses of food, tents, weapons, and direction in the field. How had it been done, back in the timeless past?

Fenelon started running the video clip of the first presentation he had attended as an employee of DataDrive. Was it Toni who had suggested it? He could see the room, see the manager at the front of it, droning ceaselessly on about something or other, he wasn't sure what. There were slides, of course, but there was too much detail for Fenelon to follow. The presenter was reading from the slides, while the audience shifted restlessly, and those in the back rows read newspapers, filled out expense reports, or otherwise found better uses for their time.

The presentation was boring, and Fenelon switched clips to one that stirred him uneasily. It was the time that he, himself, had stood in the corridor of Building Nine, waiting to present to the Executive Committee on Project Nemo. He had been up all night creating overheads, most of which were meaningless. He had simply cribbed from the files that Chatterjee had put in his office so long ago. His presentation was scheduled for precisely ten o'clock, and he was so nervous that his knees were knocking. He simply couldn't see how he, whose only exposure to the world of high technology had been the purchase of an elaborate Japanese toaster a couple of years ago, could be about to address some of the smartest people in the industry. It was like the nightmare actors have, where they find themselves on a stage, with about four thousand people in the hushed audience, and they've never even read the script once. Only Fenelon wasn't in a nightmare. Or at least, not in the kind where you scream once or twice and then wake up.

Toni had come out of the room and was telling him it was time to go in. But he didn't want to go. He was scared. She kept pulling at him and saying "Come on! Come on!"

Fenelon awoke from his nightmare with a shudder. He was sprawled out under the tree by the Peugeot. Kneeling next to him, and shaking him by the shoulder, was a stubby brown-skinned man in a Panama hat, white short-sleeved shirt, tan chinos and new white sneakers. Fenelon peered groggily around him. There was the water jug next to him. The sun seemed to be less bright. It must be late afternoon. The man was talking to him and Fenelon tried to make sense of the words, but the musical rhythm of his voice made it difficult at first to understand what he was saying. Beyond the man, at the side of the road, was a white van with the driver's door hanging open. On the side of the van Fenelon could discern lettering. As he grew more awake he could make out the words

LINGAM PHOTO AND SUPPLY COMPANY, OAKLAND, CA.

And he realized that Chatterjee hadn't deserted him after all. He had sent his cousin, who had wanted to display him and Toni Hunter in every kiosk in India, to rescue him.

SANDHYA WORE JEANS and a flannel shirt for their walk on the beach. It was summer, which meant that from about five o'clock on the sun disappeared into a bank of fog. A mist moved over them as they trudged along the shore. Fenelon carried his tattered sneakers in one hand and a jacket wadded up in the other. They had left the Chevy on a bypass along Route 1, north of Santa Cruz, and had trekked past some fields of artichokes along the cliff tops, finally finding a place where they could safely scramble down. The only other beings in sight were a man throwing sticks for his dog to fetch, and a woman sitting on a blanket, and wearing a yellow slicker.

"She's all set for the fog, anyway," said Fenelon, indicating the woman. "I hope we don't wish we'd brought our raincoats."

"I love the mist!" said Sandhya, gaily. She had let down her hair, which trailed over her shoulders, and wore a tie-dyed headband with red purple in it. It gave her a slightly piratical look which Fenelon found very attractive. "Where we live we never get this; it's either dry as toast, or pouring rain. And I love the coast, listening to the waves. They rumble, out there where the rocks are, but when they finally reach you they just hiss and run away!"

"The only bad thing about this coast is you can't swim here," said Fenelon, splashing through a receding wave. "It's ice cold!"

"I would like to swim," said Sandhya. "But I must confess, I'm terrified of the water. I mean, of being in deep water."

"You mean you don't know how?" asked Fenelon.

"That's right, I don't," said Sandhya. "My mother did not let any of us learn. Like many Indian mothers she was very protective."

"Is your mother still alive?"

"Oh my, yes! Very much so. She lives in Calcutta with one of my brothers. She is still quite young, actually, only fifty-four. But I think it is fair to say that she is already a matriarch."

"How many brothers and sisters do you have?"

"Well, there are three boys and two girls in our own family,"

Sandhya said. "My brother in Calcutta has a wife and two little children. He is the oldest, at thirty-four. My youngest brother is twenty-four. He is with Indian Airlines as a navigator and lives in Bangalore. My younger sister is still in school in Calcutta. She is studying dance, Indian classical dance. She is the baby, only eighteen. As for Ranjan, he is thirty-one. He has been here for the last five years. And I am twenty-nine. I came here before Ranjan, to get my MBA. But I told you all that at the Zilkowskis' house."

"One thing I've never understood," said Fenelon, pausing to pick up a shell. "I know these days it's not very good form to say things like this, but I've never understood how you escaped being married off, back in India. I think," and he turned to look squarely at Sandhya, "I think that you are a very lovely woman. You're smart, well educated, and you're awfully pleasant to be with. I'm certain there must have been lots of young men who fell in love with you."

Sandhya laughed, her head tilting backward, her eyes looking into Fenelon's, and her hair suddenly streaming out behind her as a breeze caught it. "You are bold!" she said. "If this were an Indian movie the heroine would start simpering and looking coyly at the hero from behind her hands. Of course, in the movies there would be some tragic reason why the girl could not marry. But in my case things are quite simple. In fact, I have been married."

Fenelon gaped at Sandhya. Finally he said "Sandhya, I'm sorry. It was stupid of me to bring the subject up at all. I'm not a tactful person."

"That is not what Ranjan tells me," said Sandhya. "He thinks you are very tactful. Here you have been friends now for some weeks. Yet you have never mentioned his physical condition to him, never asked about it."

"Of course not," said Fenelon. "I would never do such a thing. Besides, it's completely irrelevant. In fact, I never think of it at all. That's the truth."

"I know it is," said Sandhya. "You are a person who accepts. You accept situations, and you accept people."

"Most of the time that's true," said Fenelon, thinking of Jerzy and King Salamon.

"Let's keep walking," said Sandhya. "Look! We are going to get a sunset!"

Fenelon looked at his watch. "My God!" he said. "It's after eight."

They started walking again, this time back toward the cliff, next to which was the path up to the fields and the road.

"Yes," said Sandhya. "I was married at a very young age. Seventeen, in fact. I was still in school, of course. I fell in love with a man whom I met on a tennis court. He was one of the best players in India, and he was very handsome. He came from a very rich family, extremely rich. I was quite giddy at that age. Of course, my mother was against it, but I was quite determined and told her I would leave school unless she agreed to a wedding. It was black-mail. And she gave in.

"He let me stay in school, which is very unusual in my country. We had a big ceremony, of course. My mother kept saying 'and when the children come?' as if there were a battalion of little children down the street, just waiting to march into our house."

Fenelon walked, silently.

"And then the walls came crashing in, I'm afraid," said Sandhya. "I was at school, and he was traveling about the country, playing in matches. Then one day I saw his photo in a sporting magazine. One of my girlfriends showed it to me. He was walking with his arm around a woman, walking into some club or other in Bombay. I was very upset, because he wasn't there and I had no one to talk to except the other girls. I did not dare to let my mother know.

"Finally he returned and I asked him about the photo. He laughed it off with a story. And I believed him."

Fenelon said, "You don't have to tell me anything about this."

"Yes, I must," said Sandhya. "There were stories about him. One day my older brother came to me. Not Ranjan—he was in Ahmedabad, studying—the one at home with my mother. He told me that my husband was very much involved with at least two other women. He asked me to call him so that he could be with me when my husband came home. It was a very bad time for me, because we—my husband and I—were actually living in his parents' big house. His mother treated me well, for an Indian mother-in-law, but I knew she would never hear anything bad about her son.

"When he returned I did contact my brother. There was a meeting. My husband was quite rude to my brother and told him to leave us alone. He actually tried to push him out of the house. I knew there were only two paths I could take: to be a docile wife, or to leave. So I left."

"You...," began Fenelon.

"I got a divorce," said Sandhya, her voice suddenly harsh. "It was a scandal, of course. But I didn't care. I was not going to have my family ill-treated. Nor myself! My marriage actually lasted two years. My divorce was final the day I entered university."

The mist had become very thick, and Fenelon stopped Sandhya and put his jacket around her shoulders. She murmured her thanks, and he saw that she had calmed.

"I have a present for you," he said. "Here." It was the shell he had picked up and had been holding in his hand. He gave it to her.

She smiled. "I will always keep this shell," she said, so softly that Fenelon could hardly hear her over the wavelets that slashed at the beach. His heart was pounding. He pulled her toward him and kissed her.

Then, holding hands, they made their way slowly toward the path at the base of the cliff.

"I shouldn't talk about your sister and me," said Fenelon to Chatterjee. They were sitting on the log in the little glade off Route 35. "I don't want to put you in an awkward spot, but I want to tell you how incredibly happy I am. Though I honestly can't see what she sees in me. I don't mean all the stuff I used to carry around, like parking spaces and midwestern Ph.Ds and so on. I mean, a woman like Sandhya could have any man in the universe. All she would have to do is choose."

"Exactly," agreed Chatterjee. "You must realize by now that there is absolutely no accounting for the vagaries of the human heart."

"Aren't most marriages in India arranged?"

"Indeed they are, my friend. And all in all it doesn't seem that the quotient of marital unhappiness is much higher in India than it is in, say, California."

"Well, I'm not going to pursue this subject any further with you," said Fenelon. "It's something Sandhya and I might get to discuss some day."

"I think that is likely," said Chatterjee. "Please, is there any more to eat in that bag?"

Fenelon leaned forward to look. Before them on the ground was a brown shopping bag. "There's one bag of Kachinas left, and two apples and a banana," reported Fenelon, rummaging about. "What'll it be?"

"It had better be an apple," said Chatterjee moodily. "I have to start cutting down on Kachinas, I'm afraid. I have put on too much weight."

Fenelon looked at his friend and could not repress a snicker.

"No," said Chatterjee, "I am deadly serious, and you will understand why in a moment when I tell you that I, too, am shortly to engage in seeking a life partner."

Fenelon stared. "You mean you are looking...."

"For a bride," finished Chatterjee. "I have hopes of doing this in November or December—in India. Though of course everything depends on finishing Nemo in time to make the October beta test.

"Chatterjee, that is absolutely fantastic news! Excuse me, but I feel quite moved." And Fenelon gave Chatterjee a little hug.

"Quite all right," said Chatterjee. "This is California, after all. It is very odd when you think of it. There are whole nations where men hug all the time. Russia, India, many parts of the Middle East. But in this country it seems that only in California is this treated as normal behavior. Excepting, of course, athletes whose team has just carried out an important play, or scored a victory. Then it is quite acceptable, even in the midwest."

"Don't go knocking the midwest," said Fenelon. "But tell me more about your plans."

"I shouldn't," said Chatterjee. "It might tempt some demon to interfere. And, of course, there is no guarantee that I shall be successful. My education, income, and so forth would not counterbalance my physical appearance with most women, I am afraid."

For a moment Fenelon was nonplussed. He didn't know what Chatterjee was talking about. Then he said "My God, Chatterjee. Any woman would be lucky to have you as her husband. You are..."

"Resourceful and handsome and clever and popular! I know! And I can be deceptive when necessary." And Chatterjee grinned at him.

"Exactly," said Fenelon.

"Now that you are out of DataDrive, what is it you intend to do?" asked Chatterjee.

"A good question. I think I'll start looking at some of the junior colleges around here. Maybe some of them can use a free-lancer. Or maybe I can even find a full-time position. And then I've been thinking about some writing. Not that it pays anything, but it might be fun."

"Very interesting," said Chatterjee. "So you have renounced all ambition to advance in the field of software development?"

"Totally," replied Fenelon.

"Too bad," said Chatterjee. "I find that you have rather a fresh view of things that has already been of use to me. For example, when you were telling me about the Brussels sprouts... after you and Sandhya had returned from the farmers' market the other day."

"What connection do Brussels sprouts have with software development?" asked Fenelon with interest.

"You told me you had never seen Brussels sprouts on the vine," said Chatterjee. "Don't you recall how you described them to me? Fifty nodules, each on its little stalk, and each little stalk attached to the main stalk. Do you not see the relevance of that remark to project Nemo?"

"Not in the least," said Fenelon.

"Aha!" said Chatterjee.

LATER THAT EVENING, Sammi Boyadjian and his wife, Eleanor, were relaxing on their deck. Sammi was quite content with life. Dinner had been excellent, as usual. Sammi had done the cooking, which was a hobby of his. Usually he and Eleanor ate out, because they were both very busy people. She didn't have a full-time job. Instead her life was crowded with enough activities to take the place of three or four full-time jobs. Eleanor taught literacy classes two nights a week at an adult education center in San Jose, which Sammi didn't really like, because the neighborhood where the center was located was borderline at best. Eleanor also volunteered at the library three mornings a week. Her third volunteer activity was in a hospital in Santa Clara, and though that was only one day a week, it was what she enjoyed the most. Since their daughter had left home to attend the University of Washington Eleanor had missed their warm relationship, and she recaptured fragments of that feeling when working with patients and their families.

Eleanor had also gotten involved with a menopause support group and had started reading a lot about life transitions. She sometimes talked to Sammi about what she had read, and Sammi had to admit to himself that it was pretty interesting. All life's transitions were interesting, of course. And hearing Eleanor talk about what interested her seemed to provide something to Sammi that was missing in the business world that consumed so much of his time. He wasn't sure what it was, except that it had nothing to do

with politics or promotions, salaries or planning or teambuilding
or reorganizations. It was just something basic, and he felt that if he
stuck with it long enough his life would be fuller without his having to do anything else.

Sammi found himself thinking about his grandfather, whom he
had known when he was a little boy. His grandfather had told him
little about life in Armenia, perhaps because he had left it when he
himself was a young boy. But Sammi could recall a terrible and
gentle sadness that had enveloped his grandfather when he had
spoken of his own parents, uncles and aunts, and others. Sammi
had only learned extensively about his own roots quite a bit later,
and from other sources. He was proud of being Armenian, and also
very proud of being American. He was an unabashed patriot, but
his love of country was directed to something that was not a flag, or
a piece of music, or even a political system. It was something else,
something else that he would be able to define sooner or later, if he
stuck with it.

He thought about the farewell party he would be hosting for
Jerzy Bobochek and his wife. He would schedule it for about ten
days after Jerzy returned from the Great Barrier Reef. Sammi pitied
the Australians. He had several as friends, and doubted they could
cope well with a Firebrand of Liberty in their midst. They were too
suburban. The toughness had been bred out of them. But then
almost every Australian he knew was a pretty decent human being,
and Sammi was an optimist. There would be pain and suffering,
but he knew that eventually the decent human beings would win
out over Jerzy.

"Penny for your thoughts," said Eleanor.

"I was just thinking about the Bobocheks," said Sammi.

"Poor Jerzy," said Eleanor with a laugh.

"He deserves it," said Sammi. "And remember, he's gonna cause
a lot of trouble down there."

"Who's going to run the division now?" asked Eleanor.

Sammi had been giving a lot of thought to this in the last few days. He had listened to Jerzy's short list of names and had, of course, determined that none of them would get within a football field's length of the job. He had no compunction about sharing his thoughts with Eleanor, and found it often helped his thought processes to do so.

"Toni wants me to consider a young Indian engineer," he said. "He's running a big project for us right now, got about five or six hundred people under him."

"My God!" said his wife.

"I think he's too young," said Sammi. "What I hear, he's clever as hell, but I don't know how good he'd be at dealing with ExCom and the other VP's. I frankly don't think someone that young could be devious enough to handle some of the stuff that isn't in the job description, you know?"

Eleanor said "You ought to put a woman in there. How many women do you have running divisions? None!"

"I'll tell you," said Sammi. "You're right. We're kinda just starting down that track. We just made Toni a director, but out of a hundred and fifty directors we only have fourteen who are women. So we've got a ways to go."

"Well for heaven's sake," said Eleanor impatiently. "You can go outside the company, can't you? Don't tell me that there aren't any good women out there that could run that division! I don't believe it. And furthermore, Sara is a junior now and she's in computer science. Is she going to find any woman she can talk to, or use as a mentor once she gets into the job market? And don't tell me that she can go to a man. Men just don't understand."

"I won't try to tell you anything," Sammi said, grinning.

"Well, don't," said Eleanor, and she leaned over from her deck chair, which was next to his, and gave him a kiss.

As usual, Eleanor talked sense. It was something Sammi was grateful for maybe six or seven times a week, he reflected. Sammi was riding high at the moment at DataDrive. Teeny Farlow, Kyle and he were swapping insults and anecdotes. Sammi knew this wouldn't last, of course. In the high tech world nothing lasted for long. But for the moment he was doing OK. You only got so many silver bullets at his level. Sammi was fifty-two and he thought it might be high time to use one or two.

It was dark on the deck, and the cricket under it was chirping. Sammi was feeling pretty good. He said "Honey, tomorrow I'm gonna call a guy Toni knows, a recruiter named Judd. He's the guy that got us Arthur Smith. Two Arthur Smiths, in fact. I'm gonna give him some instructions myself. I'm telling you, we're gonna have about five real candidates for Jerzy's job, and three of them are gonna be women."

"Yes," said Eleanor with a small sigh, "but who's going to end up with the job?"

Sammi was quiet for a bit. "I see what you mean," he said. He thought some more. Then he said "Well, time will tell."

# epilogue

**D**EAR EMILE,

*Thanks for your long letter. Of course Sandhya and I would be very pleased to have you here, for a week or seven or eight. It's up to you. But I must warn you, there is a lot of sunlight in California. You had better bring some dark glasses.*

*I wanted to come to the ceremony, because seeing you crowned head of the department would have been a kind of closure to the academic chapter of my life. As you know, I didn't find anything really interesting here in the teaching field. Instead I am working for a newspaper, writing all sorts of articles. I cover everything from bridge tournaments to developments in high tech. I have a connection that I've maintained fairly high up in DataDrive. I mean, besides Chatterjee, of course. And that's proved very useful in getting to understand and write about high tech. This town is very small, and the newspaper doesn't get that wide a circulation, but from time to time I do some freelance work which I sell to the San Jose and even the San Francisco papers. And I'm trying to put together some kind of book that will describe the story of how I got out here, and everything that has happened to me. I don't know if it will sell.*

*Sandhya was able to move her office here without much difficulty, though there aren't too many businesses that locate on the coast. A couple of times a week she has to commute over the hill to the Valley, which would be a pain if she had to do it in the rush hour. She does most of the work from right here at home. Telecommuting, it's called. One of these days, according to what I read, all the contents of every college library will be available by computer. Imagine, Emile! You would never have to descend into the bowels of the library again! You could do all your research and writing sitting in the sunshine in your own backyard. (Just kidding, of course!)*

*Speaking of writing, I have written to Antje, and both the kids are coming to spend two weeks around July fourth. I want to get to know them, and for them to get to know their little brother. Or sister. Sandhya refuses to use technology to find out any more than that the baby is in good health and is enjoying his, or her, time en ventre sa mère, so to speak. My highest hope, my most fervent wish, is that this time spent in the womb won't be the best time in this child's life. I want to know that there will come a time when he will feel so happy to be out in life, in the fresh air, that his heart will swell, as mine does from time to time.*

*We are settling in the community nicely. I have a local dentist and a local doctor. I turned down Gopal's offer of free dental care. First, his practice is about two hours away in Fremont, and second, I don't really want him near my sensitive gums with a drill in his hand. I'm sure he's a fine dentist, but I don't think he's forgiven me for stealing Sandhya away from him.*

*Chatterjee is roaring ahead. He got a very big bonus for bringing Nemo in on time. He also got a certificate, just as he predicted, and he got to make a speech and very graciously gave a lot of the credit to Arthur. Chatterjee and his wife come over here at least once a month. She is a Bannerjee, which is almost as good as being a Chatterjee, according to Chatterjee. I think he's joking, because I don't believe that social degree means much to him. But you never know with Chatterjee. He says that eight hundred fifty million Indians in the world aren't enough, and so they are anticipating upping the number by at least one next September.*

*Incredible though it may seem, Arthur and Trudi are also expecting. It didn't take them long. Trudi is worried because the baby is due just around graduation time, and she doesn't want to miss out on any part of either experience. She's taking a year off, and then starting a master's program at UCSC. Felicia Shadroe seems to have accepted Trudi, though it took long enough. I think she is secretly relieved that Trudi comes from good Lutheran stock. Down in the valley Arthur might easily have ended up with a Thai, an Afghan, or some other flavor of the world's population. Arthur's bike shop is very popular among the high tech crowd, as you might expect. I think he's doing quite well, though if it weren't for Sandhya's insistence that he hire a good bookkeeper, he'd probably be in Chapter Eleven by now.*

*Trudi's good friend Carmelita has left DataDrive and has moved to Oakland, where she is attending classes at Berkeley during the day and is doing some freelance work evenings for Lingam Photo. I understand from Chatterjee that his cousin believes Carmelita has real talent as a photographer, and has lent her a very expensive camera, which he has taught her to use. Carmelita is about the only person around here who doesn't seem to be expecting a child. She and her boyfriend, a man named Kurt, are on the outs at the moment, and Carmelita, according to Trudi, is really going to make him squirm this time.*

*I understand from my high-up source at DataDrive that Jerzy Bobochek, who used to be Chatterjee's boss, has left the company and is now running a sheep-shearing operation in North Queensland. That's in Australia. There appears to have been a sort of Wat Tyler peasants' revolt in the DataDrive office down there, and Jerzy reportedly narrowly escaped with his life. Of course that's an exaggeration, though I do believe that it is dangerous to push Australians too far.*

*I think I've covered everyone you know about. Oh, you'll be interested in this. Shark Winfield, né Wellington Winfield, is the president of the Cercle Français in high school. Quite an honor for a freshman, he tells me.* He returned from Pau with a wealth of contemporary expressions, and it seems to have made him very popular with the members. His mother and father are very proud of him. He and I have grown very close, so close that almost as soon as he returned home he telephoned me to share his big secret. You know what I mean. And he only turned fourteen two days before he arrived in France.

That's about all from here. Oh, I almost forgot. Speaking of Chatterjee's boss, he has a new one. It took a long time, but the division has found a vice-president. Imagine! They were just coasting along for almost a year with an acting, and Sammi Boyadjian looking in every so often. It wasn't good, because the company has too much riding on a couple of very secret projects. They need full-time management, and now they've got it. Are you sitting down? She's a woman! From Chicago! Hold on, that's not all. She's black! It rocked the place. Not only that, but I believe she's about forty-five or so. That's very old for this industry, I can tell you. Her name is Markham and her background is in medical technology, but her undergraduate major—now you won't believe this, Emile—her major was French lit. Chatterjee found out all about her from Toni, who of course has access to the files. And her Senior Thesis was on French lit of the ex-colonies—what we now call the third world. That wasn't in the files. Chatterjee got it from Sammi, who got it from his wife. How's that for vindication! You were the only one in my corner on the Haitian patois issue, remember?

Chatterjee has promised to have Sandhya and me meet her soon. He got Sammi to show her some of my articles on the high-tech industry and she told Sammi I should probably be in DataDrive's sales organization! Chatterjee told me it's a good idea, and I should let him know so that he can "talk to Toni and make it happen." His words. He seems to have retained his influence over Toni, and sometimes I have an uneasy feeling I should have counted all those negatives before I burned them.

Mrs. Markham and her husband don't know too many people here, though Mrs. Boyadjian got her into some kind of discussion group she runs. From what I understand, she's tough, she plays the political game really well, but she gets a bit sick of it at times. That's rather refreshing, don't you agree?

Sandhya and I send you our love, and look forward to seeing you soon. Don't worry, we'll come get you at the airport.

Your friend,
Fenelon